Praise for *Paprika*

Frank McGuinness' collection, *Paprika*, moves, roughly, hilariously and heartbreakingly, from Donegal, to Derry, to Manhattan's posh hotels, to an apartment in Raqqa and a farm in Conglash. McGuinness knows, loves and sees this wide world and paints it with great compassion, sharp wit and always, the beautiful, beautiful sentences.

—*Amy Bloom*

Frank McGuinness has many voices, they come from the dark recesses of the heart; savage, beautiful, insistent and desiring. These stories fought their way out on to the page.

—*Anne Enright*

In this startling collection of stories, Frank McGuinness stalks through the pages like a feral cat with a scabrous wit, casually upending our notions of society in all of its manifestations, historical and modern, mystical and real, poring over the guts of humanity with a delicacy of words that will delight, enthral and terrify.

—*Liz Nugent*

PHOTOGRAPH: AMELIA STEIN

Frank McGuinness is Professor of Creative Writing at University College Dublin. A world-renowned, award-winning playwright, his first great stage hit was the highly acclaimed *Observe the Sons of Ulster Marching Towards the Somme*. His other plays include *The Factory Girls, Innocence, Carthaginians, Mary and Lizzie, The Bread Man, The Bird Sanctuary, Mutabilitie, Someone Who'll Watch over Me, Dolly West's Kitchen, Gates of Gold, Speaking Like Magpies, There Came a Gypsy Riding, Greta Garbo Came to Donegal, Crocodile, The Match Box, The Hanging Gardens*, and a musical play *Donegal* (with music by Kevin Doherty). Adaptations of classic plays include Lorca's *Yerma*; Chekhov's *Three Sisters* and *Uncle Vanya*; Brecht's *The Threepenny Opera* and *The Caucasian Chalk Circle*; Ibsen's *Hedda Gabler, A Doll's House, Peer Gynt, The Lady from the Sea, John Gabriel Borkman, Ghosts, The Wild Duck* and *Rosmersholm*; Sophocles' *Electra, Oedipus* and *Thebans*; Ostrovsky's *The Storm*; Strindberg's *Miss Julie*; Euripides' *Hecuba* and *Helen*; Racine's *Phaedra*; Molina's *Damned by Despair*; and dramatisations of James Joyce's *The Dead* and Du Maurier's *Rebecca*. Television screenplays include *Scout, The Hen House, Talk of Angels, Dancing at Lughnasa, A Short Stay in Switzerland* and *A Song for Jenny*.

Awards include: London Evening Standard Award for Most Promising Playwright, Rooney Prize for Irish Literature, Harvey's Best Play Award, Cheltenham Literary Prize, Plays and Players Award, Ewart-Biggs Memorial Prize, London Fringe Award, New York Critics' Circle Award, Writers' Guild Award for Best Play, Best Revival Tony Award, Outer Critics' Award, Prix de l'Intervision and Prix de l'Art Critique at the Prague International Television Awards.

His novels, *Arimathea* and *The Woodcutter and his Family* are also published by Brandon/The O'Brien Press.

FRANK McGUINNESS

PAPRIKA

STORIES

BRANDON

First published 2018 by Brandon,
an imprint of The O'Brien Press Ltd,
12 Terenure Road East, Rathgar,
Dublin 6, D06 HD27, Ireland
Tel: +353 1 4923333; Fax: +353 1 4922777
Email: books@obrien.ie
Website: www.obrien.ie
The O'Brien Press is a member of Publishing Ireland.

ISBN: 978-1-788-49001-6
Text © Frank McGuinness 2018
Typesetting, layout, editing, design © The O'Brien Press Ltd
Author photograph: Amelia Stein

1 3 5 7 9 10 8 6 4 2
18 20 22 21 19

Printed and bound by Gutenberg Press, Malta.
The paper in this book is produced using pulp from managed forests.

Publisher's Acknowledgements
I would like to thank Graham McLaren, Neil Murray and Fiona Reynolds of
the Abbey Theatre for their kind permission to use the specially commissioned
portrait of Frank McGuinness. I had the honour of being present when
Amelia Stein's fine photograph was unveiled in their gallery of Ireland's great
dramatists. I am proud to reproduce it in Frank's first story collection.
Michael O'Brien, Publisher

Paprika receives financial assistance from the Arts Council

Published in

For Mary Jones and Jeremy Lewis

TABLE OF CONTENTS

THE SUNDAY FATHER

My father died on the same Sunday as Princess Diana. His distraught wife rang to tell me the news. I was not distraught but I did offer her my condolences. She gave me details about the body and its burial. I listened carefully, noting it all down, for I hadn't the heart or the desire to tell this stranger I wouldn't be going.

The tickets were booked and our clothes packed before I had changed out of my pyjamas and showered. I fed our twins, Beth and Simon, their favourite mashed banana. I'd beaten the fruit to a delicious pulp. They are smiling infants except when they eat; then they look solemn as scarecrows. I've seen babies devour food as if it will be grabbed from them. Both of mine eat with no sense of hurry, sure that they will be allowed to clean their plates. That is why it took me so long to get dressed. That morning my priority was to see my children did not go hungry.

Honoria organised our usual minder. Absolutely understood she couldn't expect notice, ghastly shock, everything would be fine for a few days, a week if we liked, this wonderful woman assured us. And she was sorry to hear about my father. Yes, terrible news, shattering, quite shattering, you're so good to take both, Ria gushes on the phone. But she adores them, no trouble. When Ria comes back into the kitchen, I notice two little golden beads of sweat on her forehead. Her red hair is unruly. All done, she sighs, and leans back against the sink. Get a move on, get ready, she advises.

I don't want to get ready. It is Sunday. I want to make love. I want to throw my red golden beautiful wife to the cold ground of our tiled kitchen, I want to smear mashed banana over her hard flesh, I want to fuck our brains out all day till we have satisfied every terrifying desire and one of us is crying, sobbing our hearts out with pain. I want what I cannot have. Right, I'll get a move on. Do, do, we don't have that much time. I have a sudden idea. Maybe we should take them with us. Take the twins to Dublin.

– Why?

– He's not seen them. He probably would want to.

– You mean your father? He's dead. How can he see them?

– Must have forgotten.

– Just get dressed.

– All right.

The mourning for the dead princess I expected in London, but the Irish surprised me. It was all I heard them talking about in the airport. If they were not camouflaging their sorrow behind the newspapers, they were openly lamenting in conversation with each other. What's happened to the Irish, why have they stopped hating, Ria inquired. I could not help. I was busy wondering how strangers could be so genuinely tearful – and it was real tears I saw them shed – at the death of a woman who in life would not piss on them if their trousers were on fire. The man who bred me and left me, my father, had died that morning. I could not stir up from inside me an ounce of sorrow. How would the little princes, William and Harry, how would they manage without a mother? They have a father, I interrupted one conversation, and it must have been too sharp. For the women stopped talking and looked at me as if I had barked and bit them.

I was tempted to throw my head back and howl just to see the effect such a manifestation of faked grief would have on the two, but I resisted. What is the point of entertaining with extravagant gestures when you're never going to set eyes on the bastards again and cannot appreciate their fearfulness recollected in tranquillity? This pack of dungbags boarding our plane was driving me to demented distraction, churning my stomach into stinking sticky salted butter spread thickly on stale bread. Full of nothing but its own fat. My legs too were turning into that rancid mess, melting as we walked into the heart of the aircraft.

I would have loved to use my boot to clear off the shits lamenting Diana's death. Even to tread on their toes. To give them genuine pain. A real reason to weep. To stop their smell so that I would not have to get on the plane and be surrounded by them in that place of their excrement. Today I cannot, I must fly. Ria looked at me early that morning. You are going to Dublin. Don't try any excuses. We will be at your father's funeral. I can book tickets and pack in five minutes. That is that.

I calm myself on the flight. I imagine Beth and Simon lie in my arms. The two of them may weigh a ton together but I don't mind. Bethy always cries when we try to get her to sleep. Beth-Bethy-Bathsheba, I'd whisper. Bathsheba is what I wish we'd called her, though Simon was Simon from the start. Ria said she might suffer at school from so oddly biblical a name. I argued that it was not as if we were going to send her to school in Nazareth, so we settled on the more acceptably Jewish Elizabeth. I now adore Elizabeth because it belongs to my beautiful daughter, and for her in the future I wish all the diversities and differences her name can transform itself into – Beth, Bessie, Eliza, Eilish, Ella, Lizzie, Lisa, Liza, Eileen and a million more if she so wishes. I wonder which of these my dead father would have settled on for his granddaughter. Probably he would have called her that crying child. That eternally crying child. Put a sock in it. Take the strap to her. Slam a shoe over her arse and that will shut her crying. The slap of a slipper across her face will quieten the bitch.

Do not touch my baby. She is trying to sleep in my arms. Together with her twin brother. I will sing to them. I start to hum. Ria is curious. What are you singing? Nothing. I am embarrassed at the sound of my voice, so I sing silently to my son and daughter who are now beginning to enjoy their invisible sleep.

On wings of the wind over the dark rolling deep
Angels are coming to watch over thy sleep,
Angels are coming to watch over thee
So listen to the wind coming over the sea.

Hear the wind blow, love, hear the wind blow.
Lean your head over and hear the wind blow.

My daughter wakes up crying. The little boy wakes up too. I try to comfort them by rocking to and fro, saying, please, little ones, please don't cry, what's making you cry? They answer in voices strangely, savagely adult for two-year-old children. Beth blames me for singing such a sad song. That was what made her cry. It also turns out that I had offended Simon's sense of metrics. He points out that in the 'Connemara Cradle Song', my lullaby, I have mis-used the word 'over' three times. It is 'o'er the dark rolling deep', 'o'er thy sleep', 'o'er the sea'. This is precisely what the anonymous lyricist composed. He uses the two syllable 'over' in the last line. Had he intended two syllables earlier, he would have done so. Also the archaic 'list' is preferable to 'listen', and 'list to the wind' is more beautiful than the barbarous carnage I have inflicted on their infant ears.

I listen to this tedious nitpicking with good grace. They are still babies really. Such pedantry at that age is quite an endearing trait. Peering at me through horn-rimmed bottle-glass spectacles, their breath reeking of morning sherry, they burst into tears, having assembled about them a group of likeminded academic young ladies, sweet in blue stockings, one of whom is devoted to gathering what monies you can spare for a charity dedicated to the relief of suffering distressed gentlefolk now suffering in greater and greater numbers. Her name, she reveals, is Princess Diana, whose gentle face deserved a softer death than being squashed like a melodeon in a Paris tunnel. I can hear the crash, the car ballooning, the baying of mad dogs. Noise makes the glass of water in my hand fly from me. Luckily the spill drenches only my own person. Ria and the kind air hostess towel me down. He's fine. I'm fine. No harm done. What were you thinking of? Leave me alone, for God's sake, I want to say. Instead I thank Ria for organising all of this. She does not smile as I want her to smile. Instead, she is quite serious. She says, that's fine but maybe you were right. Maybe we should have brought Simon and Bathsheba.

Jesus, this city, how do I hate thee, let me count the ways. I hate the stench of Dublin filling my nostrils as I take the first step on this hard soil. I contain myself, I stop the smell. My brain is bigger than my body. I decide that I hate the exchange of money in this filthy temple of this filthy city in this filthy country. I suggest we pay for everything in sterling, pound on par for punt, and my wife puts me up against a wall. She declares enough is enough. These are our hard-earned wages. She will not allow herself to be ripped off, not by me, not by any chancer – get that out of my lazy, lousy head. I have put up with your shit too much already this day, she hisses. Absolutely no more. Do I understand that? Because if I don't she will get on the next available flight to London. Go back to our children. She will leave me to die in Dublin and swear to Jesus will not come back for my funeral. Does she make herself clear?

If you do not want to do that, wait for me in the bar. Douse yourself with drink. Pour the pints into you. Welcome the fountain of good old Guinness into your hungry exile's stomach. Crash into a bottle of duty-free Black Bush. Let it rip down your throat. Catch cancer hoarding the smoke of ten thousand Sweet Afton cigarettes safely ensconced in your dirty lungs. Die roaring for morphine and cursing the first Player's No. 6 you stuck into your mouth, acting the hard man to impress the harder men studying commerce. They could win over women because for some reason they had no fear of them. And you have always been frightened of women, I imagine my wife saying. That man you kept following, my boy, the man you were obsessed with, the man you wanted to fuck, what words did he use to shake you out of his spell? He spoke them in Irish. In Gaeilge. In Erse. *An bhuil cinéal eagla ort?* Is there some kind of fear in you? Fear of women. His fear, neatly diverted onto me.

I let Ria queue at the bureau de change. We get a good deal on the exchange, thank Christ. It will be expensive standing drinks at the wake and funeral. I do not know how many friends my father had made but to be safe I am expecting many unfamiliar faces. I watch my wife walk away from the counter. If Princess Diana had ever come to Dublin, rather than gallivant through Paris, now lying cold in the morgue, she too might have stood in line to get Irish money. They could do nothing for her in the best French hospitals and they could do nothing for my father in whatever hospital Dublin deigned to offer one of its least significant citizens. Blood loss stopped her breathing, and my father's heart could be cut out of his aging body and placed in her hands again, in her veins, her breasts, her child, her children. I think of her sons. The princes. Their savage grief to have lost their mother.

I think of myself. My father's son. My utter indifference. I wished him dead and I got my wish. My father that I hate in this city I hate.

Ria joins me with our money. We catch a taxi into our city, our capital, the centre of our capital. I hate the road-works disfiguring the endless detours. I hate the driver cracking jokes about politics. I don't fucking remember who the Taoiseach is. I do not care. So I say nothing. Ria says your man sounds like a right chancer. Well, he's rightly screwed us, the driver says, he's screwed Ireland. I imagine the bastard mounting the statue of Cú Chulainn at the GPO. His prick blasts through the bronze arse of the ancient hero and in juicy jubilation that cock can grow so monumental it bursts through Cú Chulainn's mouth, spouting poisonous sperm all through this hateful city, its disease of greed infecting the innocent, turning them into the guilty, the gutless, the bastard cowards that let Dublin become this hateful shrine to the shite that it smells of.

But my nose is sick of shit. I want no more of it. I want to go home. Where is my home? With Simon, my son, my loyal son. With Bathsheba, my daughter, my beautiful daughter. We're here, Ria says, we're at the hotel, you have the Irish money, pay the man! The bill is eight million roubles. Fuck it, are we in Moscow, in Petersburg, in Odessa? Why are you speaking, my good man, in that oddly Slavonic fashion? Ria pulls the wallet from my hands. My husband's father has died, he is behaving strangely. I am sorry for your troubles, the taxi man says. No, you're not, you're more sorry for the Princess of Wales, at least you know who she was. I couldn't give a fuck for her, he assures me, the English can all go to hell. I'm glad the royal family got what was coming to them. She deserved to die young – how many of ours did they take too soon? She got what they were looking for. I vomit profusely in his car, after I laugh myself sick just to let him think I agree.

He starts to scream. Bastard, bastard, get out.

He throws open the door beside me. But I decline this invitation to step outside. Instead I lean over the driver's seat and explode my guts onto where my bigoted chauffeur sat. It dances everywhere, the yellow, the green, the white, inside me, now outside. I vomit for Ireland.

He has stopped screaming. He is now crying. Big salty tears from his eyes. This fucking grown man is bawling over a car. I ask him, what is wrong? Have you lost your father? Have you lost your young wife? Have you lost your virginity? Why are you weeping and screaming as if I have defiled your life? My father left my mother and so I was defiled as an abandoned child. I recovered from this loss sufficiently well to be capable of stepping out of a cab and entering a hotel with the express intention of checking in, but my wife got there before me and did the dirty of telling them I was in need of sound sleep, that I'd be fine. Absolutely fine. I talk to the weeping driver, I say

I am sorry. You have made my father's funeral much easier to bear. I wish to give you a present. I therefore take a pair of pink socks from my hand luggage and give them to him. I tell him, in Egypt this is the done thing to thank a boy for being fucked. Or indeed for fucking. He stops crying. I smile. I say, please, for you, the least I can do for destroying your beautiful car. These socks belonged to my Egyptian father. He has just died. From an excess of pink.

Am I thanked for this act of enlightened generosity? Am I buffalo? He hurls the pink socks from the window of his car, and I catch them with the skill that surprises me. The ancient Gaelic game of hurling was never my strong point. Now, a grown man, back with his wife, having fathered two children, albeit twins, I seem to have acquired a skill, a stratagem, a structure to my physical behaviour that allows me to be so quick. So accomplished, so extraordinarily capable of playing with the profession-alism abhorred by those who know the game, who rule it, who appreciate the finer points of its playing.

Clearly my father dying has unleashed in me not so much a masculine grace but the leonine female strength of a good man with a *sliotar* in one hand and a stick in the other, arriving at that moment of triumph in a match when he becomes she and is unbeatable. I was my father's son, but when the old boy, the old fella, the old man died, I could, had I so wished, become queen of England, Scot-land, Wales, Northern Ireland – the entire territory of the

United Kingdom – should I have stayed with the treacherous, disloyal adulterer who was my husband.

Instead I married early. A virgin. I married a woman who sleeps, exhausted, in the afternoon, having gotten up early, arranged flights, dumped two kids, done every fucking job demanded of her: she sleeps beside me. What are her dreams?

She is with her husband. A drug dealer. He showers three, four times a day since he's given up heroin. He concentrates instead on selling, while all the time seeking by showering to be rid of the stench that is himself. No, that will not do. Next dream.

She mutilates herself as punishment for not having children. Her unhappy husband encourages this by sipping the blood from her wound, so purple, so lovely in the flow of juice. He dresses himself in her mutilation so he can be a man and a woman. He wraps himself in such fashion as he wishes for the cloths of heaven to swaddle round his wife's cunt and then he may not fuck her. He is thinking of his dying father. The same day as Princess Diana died. When he tries to breathe he finds her blonde hair inside his mouth. He finds a broken, beautiful body in the bathroom as he takes a piss. She is white, gentle soap in the hands he washes, pink English Rose in the paste against his yellowing teeth and the smell of woman in her corpse as he turns to kiss his sleeping wife, at siesta, at peace, in Dublin, the city he hates.

How do I hate thee, let me count the ways. I walk down Grafton Street. My, how it is changed. It is wonderful the way Dublin has turned its magical streets into my father crying like a child not to be left alone. Diana nowhere to be seen. Absolutely nowhere. I think my wife is pregnant. This would explain my behaviour.

We take the Dart to Booterstown to meet the woman who married my recently deceased father. In our pockets we carry wallets with a wad of Irish money, a little of my medication, pictures of our twins, pictures of ourselves, pictures of my father, pictures of Ria's parents, pictures of our house in London, pictures of myself at the age my father left us, pictures that go to make up life if you live by pictures. We reach the coast and get out of the Dart. I've done this before. Three times I've stood at the rusting stairway looking into the grey sea and dirty sand, wondering if he might be taking a constitutional walk along the shore and by chance bump into me. The waves would sometimes threaten to mount the stone wall and soak me, but they never did. The sea at Booterstown is well mannered. I would stand there looking out at the hard water thinking of my mother abandoned by my father, and in the seabirds' harsh voices I could hear her weeping at her cruelty in driving him away even though it was the right thing to do, for the brute beast could not keep his claws off women, any women, all women. I was once tempted to start beating my head against the wall for no good reason other than to drive my parents' memory out of my brain, but that would not have worked. I remember everything. I stand today before crossing over, looking at the deserted strand – it is always deserted – when to my shock, two horses, one white, one brown, driven by young girls, race like lightning striking the land, scattered silver beneath their hoofs, then disappear forever out of sight on their way towards the city submerged beneath black traffic.

– You could have knocked me down with a feather when I heard your name was the same as my own. Talk about like father and son. Two of them picking women called Ria. Of course I would say your full name is **Maria**. Am I right?

  – It's Honoria, actually, my wife informs.

  – How lovely. You'll never guess what mine is, so I'm not going to give you the trouble of guessing. I'll tell you straight. It's Rialto. I'm called after the cinema my mother had her first court in. Could you beat that? My poor sister, Lord have mercy on her, she passed herself off as **Agnes** but she was christened Angina. I know it's a disease, but my mother swore she was some kind of Neapolitan saint devoted to the care of the Sacred Heart. She was a cruel woman at a baptism font. But didn't we survive? And God love her, she left myself and himself lying in that coffin this lovely little house in Booterstown.

That is where we are sitting, myself, two Rias, a scrawny priest called Father Gerard and the corpse of my dead father in whose name we are gathered under this roof, hearing the click of the two clocks, watching a blank TV screen, smelling the roses on the wallpaper, the daisies on the carpet and the marigolds on the cushions. The net curtains are clean, the whole house stinks of scrubbing soap and the priest is lisping his way through another decade of the rosary. Some men might believe they have a vocation to the priesthood because of a vision, a vow, a desire to make money, a desire for security, but Father Gerard took to the collar because he was a sissy, and this vocation was as good a means of protecting his goolies from marauding boots as any other devised by God or man. He looks like a sissy, talks like one, sits like one, breathes like one. No one, as I've said, could lay a finger on him or kick the shit out of him because the bastard is both a priest and an old man. Changed times, though, in Dublin. Neither age nor dignity might spare him in this country where they've begun to hate the old and have always hated the clergy but were too tongue-tied, too servile, too superstitious to admit it.

The short silence between us is broken by the widow.

– So you have a little boy and a little girl. I would have loved a child, a girl, but himself would not hear of it. Begging your pardon, young man, your father had enough with the one. Nothing to do with you. All to do with your mother. I'm not speaking out of turn. You know no love was lost between them. But she broke his heart, and I could not heal it.

Father Gerard's voice minces its way through some observations on how many hearts have been broken by love, but if we turn fully to God he mends them, mends them all, *alana* darling. He ends every sentence with that Gaelic term of endearment. Mercifully he announces he has to be on his way. He shakes my hand, his fingers like sponge in sherry trifle. This is what he would taste like as he kisses both women on the cheeks. Sweet mother of the divine and gentle fuck, he bends over the coffin and if this big bowl of yellow jelly dribbles on my dead father's face, I will stab him and strangle him with his own pink entrails or tear the tongue from his mouth descending onto the dead flesh of my father's lined, white, hairless face. His lips reach the forehead, they touch it, they seem to linger but instead they are whispering, God take you, God bless you, God love you. And God forgive you, I add but no one takes me up.

The priest leaves. The three of us relax a little. It is clear my father's widow is glad to see the back of the clergy. She is smiling. She eyeballs me.

– Did you know your father had a great sense of fun? Especially with women. He wasn't dirty but he could make the ladies scream. I remember once in a pub in

Blackrock. It was called The Dolphin then, what it's called now God knows. Every Saturday night we had a sing-song. One evening's end your father, he hurled back his head and he roared—

Let your wind blow, girls, let your wind blow,
Throw your leg over and let your wind blow.

Then he would pretend to fart. The gang of us would die laughing.

The face in the coffin does not laugh or cry or sing. He is my father of whom I know fuck all, care less. To this old woman he is the flower of her forest now plucked and withered. He smells of orchids rare as the love between them that lasted through their life together and our life apart.

– Do you hate me? she questions.

– Yes, I did, I answer.

– Do you still?

– I don't think so, no.

– Good.

Again she eyeballs me, her blue watery pupils still capable of piercing.

– Life's too short. Jesus, look at Princess Diana, poor girl. Such a lovely young woman, her life smashed to pieces. But enough about her, we have our own grieving, haven't we? You must be wondering something. Why are we not inundated with friends and family? I know in Donegal the wakes are black with people, folk coming out your ears. You must think Dubliners very bad neighbours. Not so, my man. Your mother's funeral was like Grafton Street on Christmas Eve I'm told – mind you, she was buried on a Sunday, plenty there just going to mass. I've insisted on house private. It's looking very stuck up but when it's always been just the two of you, it's nice to spend the last hours together with no one to bother you. It's a surprise to me the two of yous came over from London, such bother and expense, but I had to tell you, for of course you had the right to see him. Should I make tea? Would you like some tea? I don't think he hated you. Rest assured—

– He broke my mother's heart.

– I'm sorry to interrupt you, she interrupts. That is just nonsense. I want to show you something. Look what I've hidden under the stairs.

She opens a press door.

– What do you think of that?

We look in and see it. A crossbow.

– Jesus Christ, Ria says, what is—?

– A crossbow. He saved up and bought it on the quiet. He'd always wanted one and a few years ago he figured out why. He imagined it must be the cruellest death, to go by crossbow. That was how he was going to top your mother off. How much he hated her. Lucky enough I stumbled on it searching for our plastic Christmas tree. That's where we stored it and I almost fainted when I came upon that contraption. I spelt it out to him. The only way he would not spend his last days in Mountjoy would be to plead insanity, and only a sane man could have managed to fire this boyo. Isn't it terrifying? Would it not put the heart crosswise in you? I'm sure he wanted you to have it. The man was never practical when it came to presents. How would you get that past airport security in the times that are in it? You see, no sense when it came to giving – I was nearly landed one birthday with an anaconda just because I was foolish enough to admire the creature on David Attenborough's programme. Again, pure luck – I found out in time and put the foot down. Me or the anaconda. Choose. Innocent he was, in that way. I know what I'll do. You have a son. I'll save it for him here, the crossbow. When he's man-big he might be allowed then to travel on planes with such things. You have a bit of a cross face on you. Have I offended you?

– How could he have hated my mother so much?

– To want to murder her? Tit for tat in a way. She wanted rid of him. She had you as consolation for his loss. In fact if you want the truth, your father told me, after you were born, she had her son and he'd done his job as far as she was concerned. He could bugger off. She banished him from the bed, that's for sure. He upped and went to Dublin. He got a job in the docks and was in digs near Monkstown. I met him through my brother. Jesus, your da was a broken piece of work then. She'd demolished him well. That bitch – don't deny it, bitch she was – she had ridiculed him into believing everything he did was wrong. Everything he touched would smash. She left him barely a man at all. I'll never forget the first time I touched him between the legs. He got such a shock I thought he'd crack in two. His nerves were shot, but I had a kind word for him and a gentle hand. It was all he needed. He was soon in my bed. We lived as husband and wife and nobody knew any different. I made a man out of the drink of water your whitred of a mother discarded.

My father continues to lie peacefully in his resting place, not contradicting her, not standing up for himself or for his own, giving nothing away as she lights four candles at each compass point of the coffin and throws a torrent of holy water onto the corpse.

– That will waken him if he's only letting on he's dead for a laugh, she says, starting to sing the 'Connemara Cradle Song' over his corpse.

Ria my wife has been saying nothing. She just eyes me like a hawk. I would like to think my silence worries her. But that's not the look on her face. Instead I'd swear she is enraged. Her mouth has the tight squeeze I loathe. It is the look of her mother watching her brothers down more than two beers. It is the look of a woman who wants alcohol but may deny it fiercely. Were I to see that expression permanently on her face it would eventually turn my heart to stone and kill me.

– If you don't want tea, how about a whiskey or a bottle of stout? It's all I've got in the house. All your father would drink. Would you like a sherry, Ria?

– I'll have a whiskey, Ria answers. And if it's all right I'll pour it myself. She starts to open presses searching for drink and finds it pretty easily.

– Help yourself, good woman, the widow suggests.

– I will, my wife replies, if I may be so bold. I hope you don't mind me being forward, seeing how you've called my husband's mother all the names of the day. But I understand how a lady like herself must have been so sour. That woman was a warrior. She tried to drive a JCB through our marriage bed. Her main method of disruption was the scare of her catching cancer. When she did die, it did come as a shock that she eventually succumbed to a strange ringing in her ears, an incessant pounding of extraordinary noises largely emitting from her heart that the poor woman insisted was moving with absolute licence through her body. She could hear it beating in her ears, her throat, even on one occasion that I witnessed myself, in her feet, causing her to dance like a being possessed in the bloodstream by the rhythm of her heart.

– She jived till she died, the widow rhymed.

– I cannot say for sure, Ria politely ignored the joke. But it may have been that exertion which caused my poor husband's mother to pass away. I believe she went cursing me for stealing her sad son from her arms, dividing mother from child as she divided father from child, but I cannot confirm or deny this ironic twist as the unfortunate matron expired minutes, yes, a matter of seconds, before we arrived in her rather impressive abode in Donegal. A self-made woman who made her pile running single-handedly the first supermarket in her home town – people used to come just to see the checkout machine. Innocent times indeed. She was well respected there, you know, not least because she dumped the useless fucker you devoted the past years of your life to serving. Weren't you the fool? Do you know, I'll have another whiskey.

Then Ria did something remarkable as she poured her drink. I was stunned to hear her sing. The first time I discovered my wife had the loveliest, sweetest, barely audible soprano voice. There she was, cradling her glass, finishing the refrains of that Connemara lullaby.

The currachs are sailing way out on the blue
Laden with herring of silvery hue.
Silver the herring and silver the sea
And soon there'll be silver for my baby and me.

One Ria joined voices with the other Ria.

Let your wind blow, girls, let your wind blow,

THE SUNDAY FATHER

Throw your leg over and let your wind blow.

Then they farted with their mouths and their faces were like bulldogs smelling each other's arses. I was visibly shaken. In my quiet way I like women to be women and from what little I knew of Father, I genuinely believe he would have agreed with me. In the day that was in it I also feel duty bound to point out that such vulgarity was not Princess Diana's way. An adulteress, yes, a foolish virgin before she married, yes, whose manners and breeding led to the bloody farce of her death, yes, but God was sufficiently enamoured of her not to leave her decapitated as it was said, wrongly, he did Jayne Mansfield in her car crash all those years ago. He must have approved of Diana, for I can remember a devout Christian of my slight, fleeting acquaintance laughing hysterically at that headless image of poor Miss Mansfield, laughing with such relish that it was clear only after the moment of her death could this sad bag of shit wank about her. Avoid such Christians and avoid all talk of Diana or decapitation of the female form when two such women are hitting the bottle the way Ria and Ria were doing. I close my eyes and pretend to sleep as they prattle.

— Has himself fallen asleep? the widow inquires.

— He might have, my wife equivocates.

— His father had the same habit, her opponent taps fingers against a glass.

– It's a bad one, my wife decrees.

– There's worse, Rialto contradicts.

– What?

– His father used to hide the drink, Rialto confesses.

– Your late husband? (Who the fuck else, I feel like interjecting.)

– Himself, she enlightens.

– You let him?

– I had to. He was a terrible man if you crossed him. (My mother could confirm that.)

– You were a martyr, Honoria canonises my father's wife.

– A martyr to his moods, Rialto elaborates.

– What would you do to get drunk? Honoria asks.

– Go down to the off-licence and buy it, Rialto admits.

– That's what I do too, she whispers.

– Uncanny, the widow returns the whisper.

– We were meant to meet, Ria, my wife, ponders the role of fate.

– Thank God I made the phone call, the widow prefers to believe in a benevolent divinity.

– He wasn't going to come, the treacherous bitch lets it out of the bag.

– Why not? (It is a challenge.)

– His dead mother, the hateful woman tells all.

– Fuck her, says the widow who did not go to finishing school.

– Our son and little daughter, sad his father never saw them, my evil wife begins to sob.

– Bless them. Does he love them?

– He loves me, Honoria is now letting tears fall.

– His father loved me, the widow joins in the weeping aria.

– And he's dead, the cruel wagon reminds her.

– She took him from me, Rialto blames my unfortunate mother.

– Who did?

– His fucking whore of a first wife. When she died.

– From the grave?

My strange wife learns of things that trouble her.

– Where she belonged. She waited. She wanted him, the widow clarifies.

– How do you know that, Rialto?

– She told him. He told me. His dying breath.

She pours more whiskey.

– What did he say? My wife downs her drink.

– She's looking, she's laughing, she's giving me her disease, the widow follows suit, swallowing the booze quickly.

– The sounds she was hearing?

My wife pours more whiskey.

– In her heart, the very same. Calling him from mine into her arms.

– She was jealous, my wife states the obvious. What did

she say?

   – It wasn't just what she said. It was the way she looked.

Rialto grows mysterious.

   – How did she look?

   – She took the shape of Princess Diana.

The widow's face is grey as her hair.

   – That's not possible.

My wife is glad she wore black as the rooms dim.

   – She kept telling my dying husband her marriage killed her.

   – Diana asked him for help?

   – She told him she had two children. He loved children, the widow sobs.

   – Not his own. He didn't love his own son.

My wife is on my side.

   – True, but he took pity on this beautiful girl and died to keep her company.

   – As she travelled across the river Styx.

   – In a boat? Rialto inquires, ignoring the allusion.

   – It must have been.

   – At least it wasn't the number 7 bus.

   – What is that?

   – It goes through Sallynoggin.

   – I don't know it.

   – Tell me this and tell me no more, the widow is testing my wife.

   – Another whiskey?

– Pour, pour, pour, she urges generously.

– What's your question?

– When I take the number 7 bus it's full of Chinese—

– What about them?

– So many Chinese people on that one bus, the widow observes.

– What's the problem?

– The bus can take eighty-one people—

– What is the matter with you?

– How can billions of Chinese fit in to the one double-decker?

– Is that what it seems like to you? Do you see them in their billions?

– I do.

– Then God love your eyes, Honoria blesses the other woman.

By this stage of their conversation I am still pretending to sleep as they sip whiskey, not noticing a strange noise disturbing the calm of the corpse. It looks as if only I can witness it. My father has left his coffin. He has heard enough of the women's endless tattle. He has decided such stuff is not for him. As he did in life, finite life, he leaves, choosing not this discourse of fair ladies as his infinity, his destiny. Yes, he fucks off, leaving those behind to manage as well as they might. The women, so absorbed in their mourning, their drinking, need not notice the dead man slipping away, no more than my mother did when he scrammed from their bed, despite my calling, daddy, daddy, where are you going? Why are you leaving us? What did I do?

If he hears us, he does not answer. If he does not hear, then he is not in this house. If he is not there, then he may not ever have been, and neither might I nor any of us. The women by this time are lighting more candles. They have started to pour Irish whiskey over the empty coffin. Ria and Ria kiss each other. They swear eternal friendship. They dance. I watch them. Then they study photographs of our children. My son is called after my father, I hear Ria telling his widow. Then they resume dancing and the tiny lad comes leaping into their dance. The ghost of my father reappears, seen by only me and my boy. Daddy lifts a candle and lets hot wax fall onto my poor little boy's fat legs. They are scarred by the fire my father leaves behind him, on my soft son, crying like a girl, like a boy, and I walk away, because to do otherwise would be to pet and confuse him.

I hear him scream too for his daddy. Father. It is the Sabbath, I cannot hold you. But I do explain to him that I have died and I have an appointment with a member of the British royal family. She too has expired this morning and by reason of courtesy, she must have priority over all common attachments. That is how things work in the country of shades. I hear my little boy say he will sing me a song if I come back. I let him sing:

The minstrel boy to the war is gone,
In the ranks of death you'll find him.
His father's sword he hath girded on
And his wild harp slung behind him.
'Land of song,' cried the warrior bard,
'Though all the world betray thee
One sword, at least, thy ranks shall guard,
One faithful harp shall praise thee.

As I listen to this childhood voice, I realise I will remember his gentle face forever, but I turn my back and beg him to forgive me, since he can never forget me. On the other hand we all have our problems. Fuck him. Sing on, sonny boy, you'll be a tougher man for it.

The minstrel fell, but the foeman's chain
Could not bring that proud soul under,
The harp he loved ne'er spoke again
For he tore its chords asunder
And said, no chains shall sully thee,
Thou soul of love and bravery.
Thy songs were made for the pure and free,
They shall never sound in slavery!

Lulled by this lament, the women now sit in a stupor. Hand in hand. They sit listening to sudden rain, glass clattering against glass. They say they're glad to be inside this night. They still do not notice my dead father has gone missing outside in the torrent flooding the dry streets, the lanes, the tree-lined avenue of Booterstown, valley of willows and mistletoe, unkissed men and women, bending the yew and sycamore, tragic creatures of the forest giving refuge to the moving limbs of my father's corpse, miraculously flexible now, stirred into his second life as animal, vegetable, mineral, drinking the earth's sustenance through the damp black and blue of the clay they might have shovelled on the pale wood of his coffin, had he not decided to do a runner. Should I tell them a miracle has occurred? A man has risen from the dead? I decide to delay the Messiah moment. They'd only fly into a panic. They'd want to search for the body. Where on earth could they begin? Where could they find him? It is the dark of night. Let us wait till Sabbath, the Sunday father passes. Then we'll see.

CHOCOLATE AND ORANGES

She looked at him as if he had been lying.

No – not lying. Thieving.

It came as a most dreadful shock. He had been well brought up. His parents, they would have been scandalised. Yes, that is the accurate word, scandalised – to think a child of theirs would take what does not belong to him.

But there could be no doubt, absolutely none, that is what Zoia, the cleaning manager, was implying. Underneath her breath, as they say here, but she was letting him know where he stood and what she made of this matter. She felt it proper she should keep repeating for his benefit so that he might not have a memory lapse in the future precisely what the hotel's policy was. All those employed here on a daily, or hourly, basis, as he was, they must follow the same rules strictly. There were no exceptions, and no favours to be asked were he to receive a call on his mobile the night before at any time up to midnight when tomorrow's schedules were complete and it was clear who needed and who did not need to show up, then he was obliged to be ready to start work at six the following morning. No excuses allowed, no special pleading – the management drummed that into Zoia's brain, and she never let anyone forget it.

Not that Ion was one for excuses nor pleading. The only time he had erred and missed a call, failing to show up eager for the fray, there was no credit on his phone, and there had not been for a few days. He had lived off bananas – a bunch, six in all, eating two at night time, washed down with milk, even sparing himself the luxury of his beloved coffee. When he had the wherewithal – how he got the cash was his business – then he retrieved the message, and he called in person to the hotel to apologise. He thought even of picking small wild flowers as a gift to soften tempers, but instinct told him that this might be a foolish move dealing with such a tough boss. The apology itself, it was received with a slight smile and a long silence. That was typical of Zoia. She nodded and sent him on his way, convinced he would never clean there again. While he was scrubbing those sinks and changing the rolls of toilet paper, spitting for spite into the bowls, he cursed each and every one of those interminable bedrooms. Now they seemed like the most desirable of residences, and he longed to open their doors again and guarantee for himself the single day's wages, amounting to a fortune when the chance to earn it seemed to have vanished entirely.

Still, he was taken back. And what for? To face the same predicament. It was not that he'd tried to skip his hours that infuriated Zoia on this occasion. But she was truly implacable in what she now demanded. That was the complete return of the tip an American couple had left in the room they'd just vacated. And he did not think that was fair.

She was not interested in such nicety. Fair does not enter the picture here, my friend – did he not realise that much? He was simply mocking her. She must let him know she would not stand for such cheek. She would not allow him dare claim ignorance. The company's rules could not be plainer. If he could not understand this English, then he should not be employed in this establishment where fluency was essential for the smooth running of the operation. The message was clear enough. Were any monies left as gratuities in bedrooms recently vacated, then all cash was to be handed over to supervisors. What those same supervisors did with it was not the business of the cleaners. So, where was it? Don't say they left nothing behind. When the lady passed Zoia in the corridor, she mentioned the tip was waiting for her. Hand it over.

Ion found himself shaking his head. He heard his voice declaring very quietly but with great assurance this money had been left for staff; that they could all agree upon without question. He was staff as much as Zoia was. But you, Ion, you are employed by the hour – by the day if you are lucky enough to be given the hours, and I am on legal contract, she protested, you have no right to tell me what I can do or what I cannot do. That money was left for me. I told you already to hand it over and I mean what I say. If you do not obey me, I will be forced to take action. I will have your pockets searched.

Now this was too much. Really too much. What was she saying precisely? Was she threatening to put her woman's hands into his trousers and remove his wallet? This was forbidden anywhere in the civilised world, and he was still a citizen of such a world even if this barbarian forgot her manners in this strange country. Had they sunk to such savagery that an act of this nature would be tolerated? It was perverse, and she knew it. I do not think you are allowed to threaten something like that, he reminded her, in case she had forgotten what a physical outrage she was threatening against him. I know you are the type who doesn't like women's hands near them – we all know that, she threatened, but I still strongly advise you to do what I tell you. I know why you have come here – what your kind are looking for. It is all you think about – so you had better watch out and behave carefully.

They had now backed each other up into a corner of the corridor. Other cleaners and chambermaids could hear every word of their argument. To a man and woman, they wanted Ion to win it. Zoia had earned herself the reputation of being a lackey for the bosses, always ready and willing to do what was best service for those ruthless bastards. She had ripped off more money than they cared to remember from those of her own who could least afford to hand it over to this painted bitch. She spends it only on make-up, on expensive wine, on the fancy man she reports us to when anyone slackens under her watch. I hate her and I hope he continues to defy her – that was the general consensus. Some even hoped he'd lift his hand to slap her face, but Ion was not the kind of guy to hit anyone, let alone a woman. My goodness, though, she was pushing her luck and no mistake when making these accusations.

Ion demanded to know what she was hinting, but she only laughed out loud. Then she delivered her body blow. Zoia told him that if he was thinking he could return to Romania and become a teacher of English in a secondary school, she would put paid to such notions – she could see to it as a matter of certainty he would not enter that profession. French is my subject, he blurted out, suddenly regretting his admission. It makes no difference, she retaliated, if I report you have been fired here in Dublin for upsetting guests with your queer behaviour, then you will never darken the door of any school back home. That lady who left the tip, she told me how you were gazing at her handsome husband. You would have made a move on him if she had not always been there beside him. Look, you're blushing – because it's the truth. I can repeat this. It will get back to Bucharest, or Timişoara – wherever your kind gather. Is that worth the price of the Americans' money? Or do you only want it because it is a souvenir of the man you could not corrupt?

He handed over the ten euro. She placed it in her purse. No guilt. She was entitled to it. A look of relief crossed Zoia's face. She even looked a little young again, when she had nearly been crowned Miss Romania. It was true – she had once been that gorgeous. But what matter? The contest was cancelled at the last moment. Some idiot official had slipped up. A clash with one of Ceauşescu's endless speeches on television meant they had to stay home, pretending to listen. She cried so much that night this was where she dated the loss of her beauty. It had certainly hardened her heart, and she was glad. For this alone she might not have fired every single shot into the fat bellies of the tyrants but spared Nicolae the husband and hideous wife Elena one solitary bullet in gratitude for their granting her a tough, rough hide to endure life's hardships.

Parting with the money, Ion looked as if he might cry. She was, however, not inclined to relent. That would have bought me food for a week, he told her. Ten euro, a week's food, impossible, she taunted him, impossible for a man with your pampered and expensive tastes. What makes you think I eat so extravagantly? He wondered.

You don't remember when I started to dislike you? she

challenged him. Why would anyone believe themselves to be disliked? he asked. But I do dislike you, she confirmed. Because I was late – I missed a day's work? Is it as silly a reason as that, he challenged her. Anyone can be late, she excused that, this is not why I loathe you. It was when we were talking at coffee about our parents. You boasted how fluent in English your mother was. She even managed, you claim, to be interviewed on British television when the tyrants got what was coming to them, telling the whole world how you all suffered, her and her children, what they suffered. Well, we did suffer, we all did, Ion argued. But how much did you, Zoia sneered. Your mother was weeping she did not have treats for her little treasures, she had no chocolate or oranges for them. How dare she weep? How dare she believe she deserved pity? How dare she think she deserved such luxury when we went without bread?

And that is why you hate me? Why you turn yourself into a thief, he accused her. Because a million years ago a frightened woman all alone in a crowd that could have turned against her at any minute, she had courage enough and was clever enough to speak on camera and lament she did not have chocolate or oranges for her children, as any mother would have complained? That is your excuse for behaving as you do, and it is a bad one. I will myself now do the complaining – against you, he threatened.

Do that, you lose your job in this hotel, and in every

hotel in Dublin. Say not a word about this, you might get a chance of more hours, but I promise nothing. That's the deal. Take it or leave it, she offered. Ion kept his mouth shut. Zoia took it as read he would relent. He was stubborn, but a hard, proud worker. A pity to lose him. Continue with cleaning the rooms, she ordered, and we will let this pass. Is that agreed? Many of those who had stopped to listen were already back on the job. Ion and the rest did the same.

When he'd finished for the day, he went out to catch the bus home. It was a long time coming. There was a small Centra shop and he went in. He wanted to buy an orange and a bar of dark chocolate – damn Zoia. He paid for both with the fifty euro note the kind couple had left behind, pocketing the change, congratulating himself for having the presence of mind always to keep a ten euro note for emergencies. A diet of bananas encouraged that thrift. The money safe in his wallet, he might even ring Romania – just to tell his mother he was managing. They could, for the fun of it, speak in English, as if a stranger might be listening, or even a little French, to keep the dream alive he might soon return.

DOMINIE

The dominie was dying, the schoolmaster Robert Henryson. That much you could say for certain. Many times he had to battle to catch his breath. But it was not what you'd imagine the sound of a man perishing would be like. She had sat with many before as they were giving up the ghost. All kinds of panic, she'd seen and heard, all screams of prayer. Pleas to Jesus, to Virgin Mary, not to be taken. Wails to mother and father to be saved – these coming from grown, strong women and men struck down in their prime. Tears in floods – spit in all directions, before a claw of ice caught their hearts and froze them, now still for eternity, their earthly torture over, their divine reward or diabolic pain commencing. Which would be the lot of this specimen? While she could not say for sure, she could still make a good guess from the way he struggled like a heathen rather than go to meet his maker. If Robert Henryson's conduct towards her, the nurse who attends him in his last hours, if that was anything to go by, Satan was waiting with his big pitchfork to toss him head first into all-consuming flames. She would have been a happy lassie to hitch up her skirts and warm her arse at that bonfire as he burned, together with his books. She hoped the devil would make sure not a word of what he scribbled would survive. Ash, all turn to ash, the best fate for it.

What made her hate the dominie Henryson so deeply? Had they been sweethearts a long time ago – her Marian to his Robin? No, not a trace of that. Had he robbed her blind, taking her to the courthouse, as the poor are always thieved from in those dens of iniquity? There they had never crossed swords. Did he spread scandal about her or any of her blood in his poetry? Not that she had heard of, for indeed had he done so, there were multitudes in Dunfermline that would be only too glad to repeat the insult to her face and watch how she would upbraid him when next she had a chance. But no such word reached her ears. Of that charge he was innocent. So, what could account for the spite, the rancour she felt souring in her stomach for the sick man?

She was not saying. That was the way she was. When her folk chose to keep their counsel, their mouths stayed firmly shut. And anyway, what would be the point of picking a crow with the feeble old fool these days? He was past caring – certainly past knowing what was going on about him. All he minded now was his insistence that a candle be burning through the thick night. If, by any chance, she doused the light, then the old temper barked once more, demanded it be blazing again, for in the pitch he could see things she couldn't. To tell God's truth, it did her heart good to watch him squirm at the sight of shadows where he could imagine – what could he imagine? His own end, and she knew it would be a sorry one.

She desired that – why? She was not a bad woman. This was not a good thing – indeed not a lucky thing either – to wish on anybody. He had served his school well. The young scholars feared the dominie's fists, but he beat the best of learning into them, that was agreed. The rich read his poetry and returned his nod, should they acknowledge each other passing in the street. His name was known to the king, it was said. There was word they might have spoken in Latin together, but what were kings and Latin to the likes of herself? She did as she was bid and minded her own business, bothering no one. Nothing scared her, for as a young woman she had endured the visitation of plague. Leprosy had scourged her. She was one of the few to survive its attentions. Her life was a miracle, the priest told her, the Holy Ghost had sang in her ear, and his celestial music saved her. She believed this. And all your days, the same priest warned her, thank St Margaret that she summoned the sacred Paraclete to you, and then she set eyes on you, to let you be healed from that most terrible pestilence. A mystical remedy. But not entirely. Her fair face was ruined now, scaled like a fish. No one would wed such an eyesore, although they would let the lazar nurse them, for she was no temptation. Since she had banished that contagion, all hands credited her with a cure, at least as far as herself was concerned. She could repulse any fever from touching her. And if they did imagine she had power to ward off all illness, she did not discourage that. She came to believe it herself. And Robert Henryson, he did not.

That was how the quarrel started, when, years before, she'd been told he was ailing and in need of a comforting, cleaning hand. He'd had the runs – nothing could bring him relief. She'd dared to show herself before the stern dominie. He contained his revulsion at the poison of her ravaged flesh sufficiently so to ask what she wanted coming to his house. She told him straight out she could aid him. How did she know he needed aiding? he asked sarcastically. I have my ways, she replied.

So you are some kind of holy fool? He jeered – or are you our wise woman?

I am neither wise nor fool, but I do not mock what is holy, for what I do is blessed, she threatened. The angels themselves allow me—

He raised his hand to stop this mad girl's ranting, warning her against blasphemy.

What I tell you is the truth, she maintained, Gabriel himself appeared and gave me power to read the ways of animals, to hear the tongues of trees, to listen to the rain and wind and learn their secrets. I tended to his broken wings. This was his garment—

She pulled from her satchel a shirt bloodied at the sleeves.

I sewed them as well as I could, she added, for I am no needlewoman, and as thanks he gave me these powers I am now willing to share with you and make you well once more.

So you have come to let me kiss the archangel's shirt? Am I to believe this nonsense? He dismissed her.

No kiss, sir, she rejoined, nor shall you touch my relic, since you are lacking in grace to receive its sanctity. I know from what trees and plants teach me how to make men conquer what infects them. Outside your door, you see a wicker tree stretch itself under the sky. That is the medicine to rid yourself of what eats you. Walk around it three times repeating this litany – wicker tree, wicker tree, will you find a cure for me—

Stop, give my head peace, he shouted, save me from such nonsense, you unfortunate, deformed creature. Quit my sight, and never dare breathe to man, beast, cloud or tree I let you say as much as you have just inflicted upon me.

I beg you, sir, listen, she pleaded—

No, good woman, he taunted her, this is what I will do instead. I will circle the tree as you ask three times, but I will make this Ave, wicker tree, wicker tree, hear my word, let me shit a good hard turd.

God heard you, Angel Gabriel hears you, she pointed at him, the Virgin hears you—

But he laughed in her face, branded as if it had been slapped with a hand of burning iron.

They hear you too, he retaliated, and they are affronted by your lies.

I am no liar, sir, what have I to gain by lying, she queried.

Then why ask me to believe you? Robert Henryson, the poet, demanded of her.

I would you should tell the king, she replied, since you and you alone of all I dare approach in Dunfermline may do so, tell the king that in this town a maid resides, untouched, beyond reproach, who would offer him service – indeed, should he ask, offer him her hand in holy matrimony, since that is the wish of his lord and master, Jesus Christ, Our Saviour Himself, who has sent his angelic messenger down to Scotland to imbue her with heavenly radiance.

Henryson greeted this revelation with silence. He did not break it, nor did she. Then he reiterated – wicker tree, wicker tree, hear my word, let me shit a good hard turd. His look through her let her know she would receive no more attention from him. And he would spread that answer throughout the town, informing high and low of her foolish cant, turning her into a laughing stock for knight and noble, slave and scholar. Robert Henryson would try to do what leprosy had not done – destroy her completely, if she would let him. She could not do that. She would not. She knew better. That was why to his shock she turned on her heel and left him waiting for her roar of retaliation. She had no need. Her hard life had taught her this hard lesson. Revenge comes at the right time.

This now was that time. He would soon be no more in this world. She could see him out of it – that much she was certain. She could tell for sure when it would come, death. Listen for the crack in the heart, hearing when it burst asunder, purple as a raw haunch of venison, ready for the ovens of Lucifer who would soon feast on its tasty meat. Yet she still could not remember exactly of what it was that the sound of his breathing reminded her. Then she knew all at once what was drumming out from that man's great belly. It was the steady throb of a woman nearing her time. Soon he must surely be wracked by the pangs of giving birth. She should have saved that news from him but could not restrain herself. She looked into his face, contorting now with increasing agony. The man of many, hateful words would be failed by his savage tongue. She could say what she wanted – he would not answer her back, not be able to utter a sound in his own defence. But she did not expect what filled her heart. What filled her, most gently, most pleasantly – it was pity. She held his gentle hand – a scholar's soft hand – and pressed it to her bosom. She whispered in his ear, you will soon get your dearest wish, my pet. Your child will soon be born. Is that what you most desire – to let it slip out of you, suckle it closely to your breast, will that content you?

In his affliction she heard him sigh, yes. I cannot hear you, tell me again, she urged, tell me louder. Yes, he bled from his mouth, yes. I cannot hear you, tell me again, she repeated. He roared as loud as he could, yes, yes. Louder, she comforted, it will ease the pain. Push, she advised, push, let the bairn be born, our dainty child, will it not be most beautiful? Will it not be most fetching? Push – then it's all done, it will be over.

He obeyed her. She smiled, wondering, who is the holy fool? I am, he told her. Who is a wise woman? Me, he cried in labour. Who is sorry now – who will be sorry for all time? You, she told the dominie, a man of sorrows, constant sorrows – that's what we will call this child, your child, pouring from his father. Shall we call him Robert? Robert Henryson? Perhaps he will be born dead. So, where will we bury him? No, not in the churchyard, he is not baptised. Somewhere outside there – outside your door, under that tree, the wicker tree? Wicker tree, wicker tree, will you find a cure for me?

She let her hand loosen. The dominie was dead. He was soon forgotten. Dunfermline had other bodies to bury, and she to nurse. Who was it spread the story she had cast a spell over the poor schoolmaster? That the devil or one of his demons was summoned to snatch his soul and hurl it into perdition? She never found out, since she did not ask, not giving any the satisfaction of denying it, for that might give the tale credence. Too many, their bellies rattling with hunger, were after the same work as herself. She would do nothing to snatch the bite out of her own mouth. On her deathbed she was left alone. The town went its own way, nowhere near her. Who did she see in the corner of her own eye but the dominie, returned to carry her, maybe on his back, to his present abode, wrap her in his angel wings and fly – where?

She thought it only courteous to inquire what he wanted. A wing slapped her hard across her maimed face, clearing it of scars, and she was gone.

HYWEL

Why have I never been to Wales? It's where he came from, and he can still haunt me. Hywel. What age did I encounter him? Finishing primary, starting secondary school? Can I remember that far back in my life? Maybe he can — maybe he has not forgotten me. How often did he come to Donegal? Once a year — summertime, blue, blue summer. His mother, she was a neighbour of my mother, who went off to work in Cardiff. She found a man and stayed. Did she endure exile willingly? Was she a happy woman, content to trek home annually for a passing few weeks?

Well, you wouldn't think so, hearing her wail setting out on the bus to Derry, carrying her, still wailing it was reported, all the way to Dublin, and then the train to the boat ferrying its miserable cargo to Holyhead. The weeping must have stopped when she stepped on the ship — she was too busy throwing her guts up. The sea made her sick as a dog, even at its calmest, she reported. She would fly if there were a plane to take her, but in those days there wasn't, and beggars could not be choosers, so it was the big steamer, as Hywel called it, or nothing.

Would she not be scared to death flying? Not a bit of it, she would never let her rosary loose, beads wound around her fingers. Our Lady would keep her safe. That's who answered her prayers for a decent man to marry. And he was a gentle fellow, soft spoken, her husband, not the type to land her with a battalion of young ones, the women agreed. So why was it, one had to ask, would you not think so from the way she sobbed leaving her home town in dear old Donegal, if life in Wales was that pleasant?

That came down to her breed. Those of her name were inclined to roar like bulls led to the slaughterhouse at funerals, weddings, outbursts at wakes, the spasms of mourning bursting from the throat of each and every grieving relation. It was taken for granted there was a bit of a want in all of us, they explained, and these ructions were our own way of going, to each his own, say nothing against anybody. Hywel's mother could bawl her eyes out then, and not a word was said, because her people expected her to do as she did. And she would do as expected, apart from emigrating to Cardiff rather than Glasgow or Birmingham.

London was considered unlucky by many people in our part of the county. This dated from the death of a neighbour stepping out in front of a bus in Putney. The university boat race began there, so it was barred from our television. This might also be why I never willingly set foot in either Cambridge or Oxford. Did he once want to study there, Hywel?

Hywel was clever, very clever, but you'd not hear him admit he wanted to be a spaceman or an engineer. When I asked him would he become a teacher when he grew up, he gave me a look of such pity that I'd date from there my resolution never to face a school room of kids. Whatever plans for himself he imagined, he kept top secret, but I'm sure they were carefully listed, for if I had to find one adjective to describe him, then I'd say he was meticulous – a tidy boy, with really good teeth.

How has he aged, I wonder. The fair hair, a single streak of dark down the middle, has it thinned as it should and fallen out, leaving him bald and pink as a flamingo? Those bright eyes, their flash of recognition, have they dimmed as dark as night, night that held no terrors for him as a child, as if no bad dreams troubled him? So I imagined, because of his smile. The smile he could turn into the most deadly weapon of welcome, has it twisted into something terrible? But I must stop. What right have I to be angry at what he could have become? I knew a boy – not this man I now conjure.

He may have changed so much – why shouldn't he? Nobody stays the same. If what we shared as young fellows was near perfect, how could it not dim and turn to dust? I should be grateful to him. In that part of the world, our mothers all worked in factories, so we were reared in our grandmothers' houses. They panicked about who we teamed up with, in case we fell in with corner boys and other bad company – then the grannies would be blamed, and generations could stop speaking to each other for what seemed like centuries.

But the summer we made friends, I waited for him to knock at that door with a lack of patience that's remained all my life. I could not wait to see his face – hear his foreign voice wondering if I was coming out to play. The most innocuous request you might say, but not if you've never been able to say yes before, because you were never asked nor wanted. His polite accent, his beautiful manners – these were his saving grace. He could be trusted not to lead me astray.

I'm telling the truth, I had next to no friends, and I'm playing no martyr. Lads sat beside me in the classroom. We chased each other around the schoolyard. Some even called me by my first name. But even back then, before our cocks had ever hardened, they sensed something different stirring inside me, and they let me know the separate ways they recognised my smell.

Young as I was, I guessed this might be risky – could turn very dangerous, when I sensed some among them – especially those most troubled by me – they might be the same as myself. Where did Hywel fit in? Who can say, but one thing I can assert about him, unlike all the other yahoos, he was not – no, he was not frightened. And for once, neither was I.

Not frightened of a football. It was only us two playing, one kicking it towards the other, not caring who scored and how many times, not letting anyone else join our game. Hywel didn't care who burst their sides mocking us. They were just jealous we had our own team with no interest in being part of theirs. Big strapping Spartans, Hywel's cousins particularly took that thick. They'd haul him to one side and whisper something about me in his ear, looking daggers drawn in my direction.

He pushed them off and told them he didn't believe that, in a voice loud enough for me to hear it. They stopped acting the cod eventually and left him alone – left us alone. Though he belonged to them, if he liked me, let him – he'd learn the hard way. But during those summers he showed no sign he'd leave me.

Together, the world was wonderful. He opened my eyes to the rivers and rocks, the strands and the mountains that surrounded this town. City boy, he revelled in meeting their every challenge, strange to him. Maybe I too was another strange challenge, and that was our downfall, I suppose. Or do I only want to suppose that?

But why should I? Did I not egg him on in all he dared? I was getting back at the brutes who sneered I was less brave than them – called me wee girl and sugar tit – they would never risk venturing as far beyond the town's limits as we did, never risk life and limb like Hywel, me watching on in total admiration of my brilliant best friend.

Hywel was his own compass. He recognised no boundaries, north, east, west and south. The townlands next to us – Fahan, Umeracam – he scorned their limitations. He even chanced the most forbidden journey by the most forbidden means – he hitchhiked to Derry and back, pining for a quick sniff of big city life and wanting to see if he could sneak into Midnight Cowboy, the film we all wanted to see then but couldn't because it had an X certificate and you had to be over eighteen.

He no more looked that age than I did, so he didn't even pretend he saw it, because he told the girl at the ticket desk they couldn't have an X film in Wales, there was no such letter in their alphabet. She told him to go off, buy a train in Woolworths, and give her head peace. Still he did make it alone to Derry, and I was in awe of him. My father must have still been driving his van that summer, well, maybe until the middle of it, and he would be at his work every weekday, including Saturday, his busiest time. It was all too likely he or one of his cronies would spot me and all hell would have to be paid for being so foolhardy as to invite murder on yourself, stepping into a stranger's vehicle.

That was before the Troubles did their damage, yet there was a kind of panic afoot, blood might be shed in

some form or other, so we were reared in unnamed dread.
I think that's what encouraged informers in our school –
so many snitched to the masters no one thought any the
less of them for squealing. I got six slaps of the cane after
one bollocks spilt the beans I'd giggled my way through
two Latin hymns at Benediction. 'Tantum Ergo' I made
out as 'Come to Margo', and wondered out loud who was
St Margo? 'Laudate Dominum' I heard as something like
hoity-toity hoity hum, so it was I found the words funny,
and was found out to disrespect the Holy Ghost. Worst
of all the teacher threatened to tell my father, who would
be fiercely disappointed by my blasphemy. No such threat
hung over Hywel. He simply could mock what he liked,
and he reported back that he was none too impressed
with the maiden city.

Derry was nothing compared to Cardiff, although he
did say he'd never seen so many deformed people. I was
too taken aback to ask what exactly he meant before he
then started running down the quaysides. These he found
a joke. There were no African and no American sailors,
not even Germans or Dutch. Everybody spoke English.
What did he expect them to speak? Irish? The big stores
sold next to nothing he couldn't find in a corner shop all
over Wales.

This was getting my goat. Did you spend anything? I
challenged him, not able to believe anyone could walk
through the streets of Derry and not be tempted. He'd

bought himself tea and sausages in a restaurant called The Leprechaun. For some reason we found that name a bit funny, and when he admitted he'd done a stupid thing – mistaking the sugar shaker for the salt cellar, sprinkling sweetness all over the chips – we laughed till we had a pain in our belly. He said even when he did it he thought it was ludicrous and started to snigger so much to himself the waitress asked him to leave the restaurant. With all eyes on him, he did so, shouting I'm mad, I'm from Wales, forgetting to pay for his food and nobody stopped him.

He only realised it a few minutes outside the café. The sweat broke on his face, and it shining with shame. He knew not to run, for then it would be rolling down his cheeks in torrents. So he walked as calmly and quickly as he could down the Strand Road until he was clear of the town centre and stick his thumb out to grab a lift, crossing the border safely back into Donegal at Bridgend.

I suppose that escapade scared him off Derry, for next he travelled in the opposite direction, toward Carndon-agh, over the mountain road. A place of desolation, not a soul dwelling there, night-time the colour of pitch, the road through it no better than a dirt track, two cars barely able to pass each other, any tractor going to collect turf causing havoc, watched by sheep who had the run of this place, ready and stupid enough to dunt any machine that got in their way since they believed they were the lords in this location. Rainbows always broke here – fragments of colour, disturbing the swathes of grey and green that alone could be seen in this barren, lovely location, lit at times by the lapis lazuli of skies reflected perfectly in the still waters of the two lakes that were the mirrors of Carn Mountain. I knew nothing about its magnificence – it took me years of wandering far and wide to realise what I had beside me, but Hywel – Hywel knew. For some reason – some instinct – in that abandoned spot he found himself in his element.

A solid week long, he wanted to head out there and nowhere else. We'd share our picnic – a can of milk with pickled onions floating in it, slices of bread with purple blackcurrant jam, and a bar of Cadbury's chocolate, stuffed green with sticky peppermint cream. He got the beginnings of a tan, I burned like a beetroot, for each day that summer the sun beat down, I seem to remember, as if it blessed us.

Just as well, as there was little else blessing me at that time. I had started doing badly at school. In those years teachers casually, brutally beat children, believing that pain was the greatest incentive to learn. I didn't want to get hit, so by and large, I knew what stuff we had to recite by rote. Being too much of a coward just to let this happen, what in hell was stirring within my brain to make me disregard all threats of punishment? My laziness was not in the hope of attracting attention – that much I swear to – but I just stopped preparing homework. English I could do in a flash, no bother – though geography, history, Irish, sums – subjects I had to knuckle down and get crammed into my head, these I made no fist at, and I couldn't figure out why.

Pupils would line up around the room's four walls, the master would quiz us, and in the middle of one such interrogation, he moved me straight out from the smart row into the slow one. It was the first time I felt a person take pleasure in cruelty. I had been stumbling to find some sort of answer – a Gaelic word that might correspond to an English one – when he suddenly, calmly told the students, to take a good look at this stupid donkey. I was no better than any of them, though my people might think differently, but watch what can happen – the mighty have fallen. My like were no better than the lowest of the low.

To their credit, not one looked or laughed at me, although I know my cheeks were scarlet. We had been shamed enough, most people in the town concurred, and their children followed suit. Not the man though who felt obliged to heap more ignominy on my head, and whom I cursed there and then. Did harm befall him, or any belonging to him? Years later I discovered his wife had chastised my brother because he played hurling in front of her house, telling him his mother would be better fit inside her kitchen minding her young ones than out gallivanting working in the shirt factory. He thought it better to keep that to himself, thank Christ, for if he'd mentioned it at home, my ma would have stuck the hurley where it should have been stuck up the witch. Maybe that's proof such curses are never heard, or so I've been told.

Hywel though was always top of his form – that's what the Welsh called their class year. Form. His mother loved to hear him recite poetry – Wordsworth, Tennyson – even his own, she confided to my mother, who said she only wished I would or could say my prayers on occasion. An ear untrained to the subtleties of our spiritual finesse might read this as a dig against me, but it was in fact solidly directed at the other woman. Hywel's mother had married a convert.

Let her parade him to Mass and Holy Communion every Sunday of their visit. Let her brag he knew more about the intricacies of the Catholic faith than she did, or indeed all the priests of the parish put together. There were still those about her who, in small but savage ways, could never allow her to forget that because they hadn't seen him personally at the baptism font, they could not credit that the man was now digging with the same foot as themselves.

If he really was one of us, why in Jesus' name call their son a name like Hywel? His parents took every opportunity to explain this was a family name – that's what his father's father was called, it was indeed quite common in Cardiff. Although smiles were sweetly exchanged and heads softly nodded, this excuse cut no mustard in certain quarters. I don't think I'll live to see a Pope Hywel, one neighbour intoned, but then she swore she'd never recover from the shock when she heard one local family had the cheek to call their daughter Marina. She claimed that was the name of a breed of sheep, forget any palaver about there being a princess of the same title. Anyway, despite this begrudgery, Hywel was a smart fellow. Though he tried hard not to, he could not always stop himself letting me know it.

We had the Atlantic around us on all sides, but we tended to stay clear of the sea. I had a cousin who'd drowned when he was only four, rambling down a laneway, falling into the water, washed up the next day – a terrible tragedy. We were then forbidden, absolutely forbidden – each and every one of us – to go near the shore unless we had a grown-up with us, and then it was to build castles made from the white sand. Swimming was out of the question, for although it was never explained, there was a consensus that our ones suffered a bit of a lack of wit when it came to the Atlantic Ocean. It could talk to us and make us do what it bid. So we vowed never to listen to or go into it, and not to break that vow for love nor money, which we didn't.

I explained this to Hywel, half expecting him to mock me, but he agreed you should honour such an oath when you take it. It was the same as service to your queen or king should you enlist in an army. Not that he was going to do that, although his dad served in Cyprus for a few years. Hywel could swim though – he'd learned at the baths near his house. He'd enjoyed it. Enjoyed it a lot. That's why he was so tempted to leap in one blistering day, looking at the cool, cold waters on Carn Mountain.

Tomorrow though. Not now, not this minute. I was glad. Water petrified me so much, I was shocked to the core seeing people in it. I could scarcely move till they were out again on dry land, towelling themselves dry as cucumbers. When did we first see a cucumber? As rare as red peppers back then. Salad was a slice of ham, a leaf of lettuce, a trace of tomato, a yellow sliver of egg, nothing else. Who would want to eat it? It was as good as going hungry. And what was the point of starving yourself? None whatsoever. That is how Hywel's voice comes back to me, for some reason. He said if I liked, he could always do as I wanted. What did Hywel sense about me? Something that stopped him leaping into the lake as he promised? Was it a touch of nerves?

I can't say, but that day something had happened. He was really silent on the long trek back. No cars halted, which was a bit of a surprise. That beautiful smile of his put the brakes on nearly every vehicle that passed, be it driven by a young or old man – so few women were behind the wheel then they were a rarity and they were warned never to pick up passengers of either sex or any age, so they just didn't. For once we were out of luck this time, as we began hoofing it home. I'd hoped he might start impersonating his Irish relations which he could do to perfection.

We'd devise scenarios where his Donegal granny became a Bond girl to my Sean Connery, insisting he wear a woolly vest to save him from all harm on dangerous operations. He'd memorised whole chunks of the *Carry On* films and delivered them in a variety of broad Welsh accents. He had me pissing myself at his Kenneth Williams digging coal down a pit and still keeping himself immaculately clean. Sometimes he'd pitch his voice really high and mimic Mary Hopkin who won the talent show 'Opportunity Knocks' millions of times – 'those were the days, my friend, we thought they'd never end.' That was her big hit, and Hywel had it down to a T, even pretending to toss her fringe out of his eyes and strum her guitar.

I was the only one in these parts to find this comical – his cousins thought it certifiable – and I wondered if he practised routines on his own to impress me. There were none on display this hour, the pair of us walking along not speaking a syllable, until out of the blue he inquired, why do you never do anything together, you and your father?

Nobody had ever asked me such a question – so I genuinely wanted to know why he was asking that. I forgot to be on my fiercest guard whenever anyone fished for even the smallest bit of news on that quarter – that was why I took the bait he was dangling.

–You and your father, I never see the pair of you doing things in each other's company, I'm wondering why, he concluded.

I dredged for the best I could throw back. The same could be said about himself. Not in Ireland maybe, he retorted, but in Wales the two did, they certainly did, they went to rugby matches. We don't play rugby in Donegal, I pointed out. That's a pity, it's a good game, he observed, you'd enjoy it. Why? I wanted to know. You just would, he smiled and left it at that.

The smile – the same smile – never left his face the following day either, though he made no mention of rugby, nor, more to my relief, my father. I thought the light had started to fade as he began to take off his clothes to go for a dip, but that might have been just a trick of my eyesight, for I had been well trained, as were we all back then, not to look at anyone in any stage of undress, as if naked flesh could strike us blind on the spot were we to do so much as glimpse it. I did not gawk at him as I heard him remove his shirt and shoes, and that might have provoked him back into the subject of my father, but now, to add to my distress that I might witness his bare body, Hywel wanted to know exactly how close to the edge of the pier my father hovered and for how long?

The shock nearly choked me. Of all the stories upcast to us, this one I'd never suffered. That barren mountain of gorse and rock had turned red with my scalding tears as Hywel kept stirring his poison, asking, insisting to know.

– Who got your dad out of the driver's seat?

– Was he crying as he sat there, threatening to drive into the Atlantic?

– Did your mum watch it all?

– Did she do her best to persuade him not to carry out what he threatened?

– What did they do to his van when they managed to get him out safe?

– Was he taken home or into an asylum?

I nearly blurted out my father never went into such a place, stop this interrogation, but something silenced me from speaking, even gazing at him standing there, near bollock naked, inviting my eyes – to do what? Enjoy him? My hands to do what? Slap him across his dirty lying mouth? But for all I knew, what he said might not be lies. Might be the truth. I didn't want the truth. I wanted Carn Mountain to open up and bury me. He whispered in his softest voice had he asked something he shouldn't? Why wouldn't I answer him? Why wouldn't I look – look in his direction?

So I did. He was dressed now only in black boxers, with large red roses covering all over them. Do you like my shorts? he asked. My mum bought them, two pairs. Would you like the other one? My cousins think they're really cissy, but I like being a cissy. Do you?

I didn't know what he wanted me to say, but in some vague way I realised this whole scenario was connected to my father, and whatever I said would be used against me. I suddenly thought, seeing him like that, he looked ridiculous, like a clown, his beauty painted on his lips and cheeks, the red roses he was wearing blood from his white cock and arse, buried in black, wanting me – wanting what? To do what? Remove his underpants and don them myself, leaving him stripped and powerful, and me as ridiculous, as clownish as he was, now when I would not obey him. He wanted to know, what's wrong? Are you frightened? Do I scare you or something?

I couldn't tell.

I wouldn't tell. I just shook my head and walked away from him and all belonging to him.

Did he call out to me, it's only a joke. Did I hear a splash as he jumped in? Let him sink or swim, I didn't care if he hit the bottom. I kept remembering all the times we tried to skim stones over the top of the lake, but we never once succeeded. There must be a knack to it, but neither of us possessed it.

I walked home, a pain like a stone in my gut, knowing for sure I would not set eyes on him for the rest of his holiday. Hywel made that doubly certain. Next morning his mother arrived at our door, her face like a fiddle.

Her son had arrived home on his own very late, his good underwear drenched beneath his trousers, she said. I'd pushed him into the lake, wrestling beside it. Boys would be boys, she accepted that, but this was damned dangerous play. He didn't want to change out of them in front of me, he told her. That's when her tone changed.

She started hinting there was something not right about this whole business, something strange about me – maybe my mother should look at her son as a very odd kettle of fish if this lark was what he got up to. In that case, it takes one to know one, my mother reminded her. I see, she said, well, if your lad's not normal – and at this we detected a hint of Welsh in her accent – he didn't lick it off a stone. Is it any surprise that in a family that's always drowning, they should try to drown other people as well? Fatal, that's all you are, the whole shower of you – fatal.

I never set eyes on Hywel again. The next summer his whole family went to Cyprus, to visit the war graves of his dad's fallen comrades in that civil war. They found an excellent hotel, the weather warmed them, so it was decided they'd return the following year, and thus it became a habit. I don't know what stories of his dad's exploits were spun on these trips, but they must have had their effect. I kept hearing how well Hywel was doing at school, but then the big shock – he did join the British Army.

His father was delighted. It would knock him into

shape and keep him on the straight and narrow, his Irish granny confessed, for he had started mixing with a wrong crowd. It meant he could never come back to Donegal, of course – too near Derry, someone would take a pot shot at him. His parents shouldn't risk it either, but they did for the funerals when each grandparent died and was buried.

Even then, Hywel couldn't visit. Wasn't it an awful thing a grandson couldn't pay his last respects to his own flesh and blood? Wasn't it a terrible politics that allowed this kind of hatred to fester? What was the world coming to any road?

Nobody could tell the answer to that. Hywel was very likely never sent to Northern Ireland because of his family living so close to the border, but who could tell? I presume he survived his time as a soldier, for we never heard otherwise. Then, maybe we wouldn't, and who knows what secret ways the military works and hides everything? When I'd listen to the news for years after, throughout the Troubles, on BBC, and they announced a killing in Belfast, anywhere in our part of the world, I admit I always hoped it would not be Hywel. To my knowledge, it never was. That way then I was free from all suspicion that I could, by any means, visible or invisible, have pulled the trigger.

THE WIDOW'S FERRET

She disliked animals. They had their place. Not in her home. They were not welcome. They could be responsible for fleas. Fleas were an affront to any civilised person. This was not being swanky or rare. And it would take a rare man or woman to have sex with a ferret. She was not that rare, thank you very much, mister.

She said that sentence to herself, and she really had to laugh. It sounded so northern. And it had stopped sounding foreign. She had lived in this area so long you'd swear the strangeness of its sounds would not matter – would not make her cry – and it didn't. She now loved this place. If they showed John Betjeman's documentary on Dublin's architecture as an archive treasure on the BBC, she did not get on the first bus south the following morning. People were friendly in Coleraine. They were so kind. She did not even mind the many silly suggestions that she get a pet. She resisted – she bit her tongue instead of telling them to go fuck themselves. In the silence she once nearly tasted her own blood in her mouth.

She should not have taken the advice so seriously. People were ridiculous, but it was understandable. Men especially, they meant well. Cautioning her to go for the best – buy a pedigree dog or a finely bred cat. A cat particularly would be company. For her, cats brought to mind Egypt. Armies of them, guarding the pyramids, or marching in phalanx through ancient cities of Mesopotamia. Lovely names, Ur or Baghdad, like a mouse in a heaving paw, flattened, eaten. Had she been fighting the Iraqis, she would have come across weapons of mass destruction. Even one would have been sufficient. She was not a greedy woman. She had always been lean as a greyhound. A whippet. A well trained thin spaniel smelling out bombs on the platform of Belfast Central Station. If she had been turned into an animal – she would not have wasted time smelling her own shit, depositing her piss about the streets of Coleraine. No, she would have hastened to the centre of conflict, carrying that particular device which could destroy the entire feline population of this town. Not the people nor the buildings. They would, like herself, be left standing. Trembling, traumatised, but still on our feet. And of course she would spare the bridge over the River Bann that cuts through the heart of Coleraine.

When she first moved there, one drunken neighbour whispered a terrible secret. He was a well-known queer, always after policemen or rugby players, a red-faced ghost she thought him, renting out rooms to students, most of whom he sucked off in lieu of rent. That's what the word was, she saw no reason not to believe it. Nor did she not believe him when he whispered that if civil war ever does break out in this province, you're stuck in the worst possible hole for a Catholic to find herself. I beg your pardon, he simpered, I know you've shifted sides – since you tied the knot, you're now crossed over to our ones – but I tell you, some are savage, and if they ever indulge their blood lust, if they free their fists from beating the bastarding drums, they'll tear down that bridge and cut off each and every Fenian or Free Stater from escape. No one will be able to do a runner. They'll shred you to ribbons – I'm warning you.

She looked at this man as if he were mad. How long since she'd been called a Free Stater? The red ruin of his face matched the red of his tie. She made no acknowledgement of his nonsense. She simply vowed she would never drink in any pub in this quarter ever again. She kept her vow. But in the dark days – even before he died, there were dark days sometimes – she thought of that bridge. She saw it demolished stone by stone. Men, women, children, bound hand and foot, green ropes paralysing them, blood from their mouths hurled into the innocent Bann, the river weeping to receive them, trying to soften the blow of their death at the hands of their neighbours, drowning them as swiftly as possible, taking the little ones

– stop this now, stop. Only being silly.

Silly and stupid. Deeply ungrateful. She lived surrounded by friends and acquaintances. A lot of her neighbours were in the police themselves. None of them were widows but they would surely never see her harmed. They were friendly. Friendly as could be. Sociable. But those who had mentioned the cat – she wished they hadn't. Yet they kept on and on, bringing back to her time after time school books where she read of cats worshipped in Egypt. She never got that out of her head. It just stayed there. Don't imagine she ever went to that pagan country. Still, she was always there in her daydreams.

God's curse on daydreams. As for night-time – it was fine if you could sleep. She couldn't. So often she just could not. She'd lie awake letting the most ludicrous things slip into her mind. It had happened on so many, many occasions she stopped trying to control – let it flow – no harm to it – anything to stop seeing him dead. It always happened at three in the morning. That was when she'd imagine skiting off to Egypt, landing there, not letting herself be scared to death, doing the sensible thing, covering up completely, bandaging herself against the utterly destructive heat of the sun. It ate you up. Everybody knew it dried your skin, but it also drank your bones. The sun fed on your marrow. It took its pink and turned it into gold. The sun spent your gold like water. She never went out into its heat, day or night. That was why she was intensely white, completely immune to the melting temperature of Thebes, of Coleraine, of Egypt, as she walked along marvelling at the sights and sounds of this civilisation, when she suddenly realised she was carrying on her person, hidden in her handbag, a machine gun.

Wherever she found idiotic Egyptian folk on their knees praying to a cat, she shot them. She'd search for something the heathens believed she was looking for, say a compact to powder her pale skin, the compact in the shape of a crocodile – had she thrown it at them they'd scream and step back, imagining it might bite them – but no, out of the handbag came a weapon of sufficient destruction, and she blasted them. No mercy, I'm afraid. She was utterly cruel in that way. She'd learned to be. Even if it was only in her dreams. Had she ever been transported in person to those faraway, foreign places, her weapon would have been money in her purse. Bestowing it would have seemed like a miracle. They would have proclaimed her a goddess, ascending into heaven. But she would have kept her bearings. She would have ended back in their own bed. Where she slept with him. Without him. Ronald. Who believed—

What did he believe? That they would be safe. She would never be without him. She would never have to resort – what was it she would never resort to? She couldn't as yet say. Nothing could be said. Never answer how they expect you to reply. Leave them wondering.

That was the way of working in this part of the world. So everyone believed. She didn't. She found the people very direct. Straight. Look at the lovely row of Georgian buildings down at Hanover Place. They were simply demolished. The council had put a protective order on them. The builder knocked them down. There were a few who raised eyebrows. A string of letters in *The Chronicle*. But they were gone forever. Who missed them?

In her way, she did. Her first hairdresser was in one of those buildings. Tina's. She chose it for no reason other than the name. Neither one tribe nor the other. Innocent. She liked the owner, a Limavady woman, two kids, husband drove a lorry – his own business. In all her years going to get her hair done she had gleaned only that from scraps of conversation.

OK by her. Tina could do her hair well. All that mattered. But her head grew a little sore, strangely sore, when she was told this would be her last visit likely to the salon. No more would she push open the maroon front door. Glance in to see if anyone had taken over the bankrupt solicitor's office on the floor below the salon. There was a big poster of Rory Gallagher peeling on the wall, his guitar elegant in his hand. The boys on the bus coming home from school loved his band, Taste. Practising his blue songs, making the words more indecent, they used to tease her, once asking what Rory could sing to shock her. She had a piece of chalk in her schoolbag. She took it out and wrote, on the back of the bus seat, Thank Christ for VD. I'd like to hear him sing that. They were shocked. One of them put spit on his hands and rubbed it out. She was rarely bothered again on the way home, though now her nickname changed from mousy to scabby. She looked at Rory Gallagher and smiled. For old times' sake she scratched the guitar peeling on the wall. She wondered what had happened to those lads who'd tried to torment her all those years ago. Dead maybe, married, fled some-where, to the States, to Spain, to Majorca. That was where he'd done a runner, the disgraced solicitor. No one else she knew had ever done that. She wished the cheating robber well. It was only money he took. But now it was time to ascend the stairs – rickety stairs they were, ready to collapse. She thanked God she wasn't a heavy woman.

She wanted to take up a question with Tina she'd not dare answer – not dare ask – before. What would Tina do if there were ever a fire in this house? It would go up like a matchstick at the hint of a spark. Tina laughed. She said she'd throw herself out of the window and into the Bann. Her assistant said – she joked that if Tina were to dive into the river, the size of the splash would put out the flames of the fire imagined in the salon. Tina roared laughing. She called the girl a bad bitch. Tina was the boss, but she could take a joke – she would give the young one the road, if they weren't all for the push.

But seriously, the man upstairs – they were soaking her hair. He must have been four storeys up – I will die gasping for breath as they drench every root and residue of dandruff. Tina knew for a fact that he kept a rope – a big rope tied to his bed. She was released fresh from the basin. If something did happen, he'd climb out and down the building. If she had vomited while her head was held back into the drenching basin it would not have been funny. Woman's windpipe torn by her own puke. Stop thinking about yourself. Think of the poor man suspended by his rope while fire raged. The blaze might devour him. He could easily burn to death if that was all he planned for his safety. But you could not talk to him, he was English. They knew it all, didn't they? Tina concluded.

Straight away she was imagining the poor man swaying on his rope, his pyjamas singed and torturing him. Maybe he slept in the buff. So long had she not thought of a naked man she actually blushed under the dryer, feeling the skin of this fellow, the fine hairs on his English arse, his sweet purple cock. God forgive her, this dying creature was a human being, and all she wanted to look at was his private parts. Dirty bitch she was. The assistant shocked her out of her pleasure. Did she want a cup of tea? No.

When she took out her money to pay, Tina closed the clasp. She was a bit taken aback – it was as if the cash was going to be snatched. Of course, the opposite hap-

pened. The kind woman was saying, You owe me nothing
– nothing – not this time. I've valued your custom. In all
your years coming here, you've never taken as much as a
drink of tea. This is from me. There was no danger of the
woman kissing her. Not done here. They shook hands
and wished each other well. It was as she was leaving she
noticed a bundle of stuff packed in a big box. At the top
of the mess there was a tiny statue of the Sacred Heart. So
she found out at long last. Tina was a Catholic. And she
still had some generosity to show for the turncoat widow
of an RUC man. No – no tears, not a chance, not after
so long. But she found herself looking back at the two of
them – I'll miss you, I will.

What had possessed her to say something so stupid? The
women looked at her as if she was – what was she? Some
kind of tinker woman who was begging for a free haircut?
She could feel lice on her scalp but she would endure the
itch and not give them the satisfaction of scratching the
vermin. Did she smell of smoky gypsy clothes? Were they
expecting her to pull a shawl from her bag and throw
it over her stinking head? Was there something in their
minds that she needed – no, it was worse – she expected
charity? She took eight pound coins out of the purple
purse – purple like him hanging there – control yourself
– but she couldn't. She started to laugh as she counted
out the precise amount it would have taken to pay for
what she owed. She watched them watching her, shaking

their heads. She placed the money on the chair she sat on. She left them saying nothing, not looking back at them mocking her, the poor, deserving, dirty bitch. She banged their door shut. Climbed down the shaky stairs. Wanted a cigarette. Drop it on the ground and rush out before the stairs burst into lovely flames. But she didn't smoke, she never had. What was she thinking of? Could somebody be kind enough to let her know what?

The fresh air did not settle her. She didn't want to be settled. How dare people make any kind of concession to her. They all tried to do so. They all seemed to be in the know. Except herself. Something was afoot. She was not party to it. What was it? It seemed that people on every side of the divide were suspicious of happy marriages. If you loved your wife, it might become a rule of law that you were certain to get it in the back. It was always the good and loyal that got plugged. You heard it every evening in the news. It was beginning to dawn on her that maybe they were all in cahoots with the murderers. She could not bring herself to admit what she'd long suspected. RUC, IRA, British Army, UDA. Fuck it, the whole shebang in Northern Ireland – it could all boil down to a very effective way of making sure you don't need a divorce. Everybody is killing off an unwanted partner. That is why murders go unsolved. They are all in this together.

She was putting such things behind her. Slowly but

surely. It was a kind of grief. She wouldn't excuse herself like that. She was ashamed for entertaining notions that such baloney would ever be true. What was she becoming? Ronald would be – he would be understanding. All the more reason to get a grip. Keep that grip. Firmly. Such rubbish about divorce. It was something left behind to fester from her rancid Catholic childhood. Against her will, she was still controlled by the catechism. God made the world, God is our father in heaven, we should love God above all. Her world had broken into bits, no one heard her crying nor helped her on heaven or earth, and she had loved her husband above all others. She had committed the sin of pride – why could she so exactly recollect those ridiculous lessons? Warped, hateful. She had to leave primary school behind her. She had to grow up. It was time to take stock and see the good side. Be sensible. It was sensible to remember that many people change partners. It can all be for the best if a marriage were to end. The new couples that create themselves after they separate, they can even meet without a battle, particularly if there are children. If the worst comes to the worst, they can rise to an exchange of pleasantries.

But her marriage had not ended calmly and legally in any court. No. He was blasted to kingdom come. The vision turned her stomach inside out. His face – what face he was left with, it was a stick of stewed rhubarb. His eyes were custard. She insisted on identifying her husband's body. She smelt frying off his flesh. It was as if some god had wanted him for his dinner and dessert. But the touch electrocuted him. Left him near to a cinder. Now, he was discarded, bone picked clean down to pink marrow, waiting to be shovelled into the earth of the province he died defending. All she said on seeing him was, here is the man kissed me this morning.

She was declared to be a brave woman. A tough lady, some judged. She'll survive. She never cried either. In fact she was always on the verge of bursting out laughing, as she'd done – wherever it was she'd last done that. It was one of the reasons she avoided cafés and restaurants. It was not that she was in purdah. It was just that any mention of the Ulster fry made her want to giggle, want to accuse these people that they were a gang of cannibals. You are damned in this country because you eat your own. You down the blood of your brothers. You devour your sister's skin. She had, by necessity, to keep her mouth shut. And so she never smiled. Never gave interviews. She was asked to do photographs with others who were touched by grief. By disaster. By murder. She was not that keen. The government understood, but could she not reconsider? The police would put no pressure, but did she not realise – I'm afraid I do and I don't care, let that be an end to it. An end to it now, she insisted. She always fiercely refused. The mood towards her changed. The tough lady became a hard piece of work. The brave woman was maybe a wee bit selfish. Too fond of her own mourning. Too much harping on her loss, after a certain period of time, well, for want of a better word, she was spoilt. Some called her heartless.

She could immediately scan her own body and watch it without a heart. A beating heart. Instead it was lying quite daintily, quite deliciously, on a white plate beside her. Dainty in that it was so small. Delicious it must be, for there was a knife and fork set prettily beside it. Someone must have cut it from her, with the precision of a surgeon, as she slept deeply for the last time on the night her husband was being blown to the four corners of the earth in a nondescript village no one had ever heard of before or since. What clever engineers those bomb makers proved themselves to be. How expertly their fingers had constructed such a truly sophisticated piece of work. In the very instant they dismembered three living men, miles away, tens of miles from the epicentre, a shard had travelled through the stench of the air, breaking its rotten eggs, and that shard jagged her, entering the breast of one wife. Maybe it even entered through the finger, the imperceptible space between flesh and wedding ring. It exploded inside with such remarkable energy that her heart had cut itself cleverly from her, and she was left to live without this vital organ, keeping alive by supping daily on the merest fragment of that food placed so considerately on the white plate, knife and fork neatly folded over each other, waiting for her to dine. If she ever met Ronald's killers, she would amaze them when she thanked them for the delectable sustenance they had so unexpectedly provided her. This would be immediately before she disembowelled them.

She could get away with that, she reasoned. Walk off, unidentified, scot-free. No one could trace her. Not even the most complete police procedure. To hell with DNA. It had no fear for her. And here's a good one – here's one to make you howl – take this on board, boys – it was the killers – they were responsible for this extraordinary gift. If they had left her a heartless woman, they had also made her invisible. She could have marched for miles, walked through walls, without benefit of arms and legs, without breasts and head, hair or feet, if she could survive without a heart.

This power pleased her. She wondered would Ronald have fancied his invisible wife. Would he have found the space where her ribs had vanished, the vacuum in the centre of her face, the hole where her tongue should be – would he have found her repulsive? As his body had turned to meat and jelly, now her body was nothing, without stain or smell. What wickedness worked its magic on both of them? Wife and husband were transformed entirely, transformed beyond recognition. Taking to an early grave, one was put in the earth. The other took to the sky. She realised that if she so desired, she could spread her unseen arms and fly. Dear Christ, she could fly. But this was to be resisted. Resisted for a reason. And it was all explained by a comic book she'd read as a girl.

She remembered that specific story in *Bunty*. This was about a disappearing schoolgirl. Her dad was a scientist who'd discovered some miraculous potion. It was for the British military's use and was only to be employed for world peace. Wasn't he – the father – kidnapped by foreign spies? His daughter alone kept a sample of the elixir. Only she could free her father – she drank it and could vanish. But who would believe her? She realised she had to ration the magic. If she swigged a few drops only part of her vamoosed. To prove this, she did a strip in front of her friends. Her head and legs were there for them to see. The rest of her was hollow. Her clothes were covering nothing. There behind her pink bloomers and black schoolgirl boarder stockings – nothing, nothing at all. A blank body.

She had never seen knickers of any shape, size or colour in *Bunty* before. Maybe it turned her on a bit, she was just hitting puberty. But it was as if in losing her stomach, her arse, her woman, her knees, the girl was so misshapen as to be something alien – even something beautiful. And her name was Ira. Honest to Christ, that's right. She could not make up such a connection. Had she read in that child's comic some hideous prophecy of what would destroy her life? Not merely would she lose her husband, his body, his soul be taken, they would also want to take something more from her. In making her invisible they wanted her to cease being a woman. No man could literally set eyes upon her. No man could find her attractive. The only ones who would have done so were the bastards who killed her husband. Those malignant eunuchs would have been enthralled to remove her from womanhood. It was this which convinced her absolutely that the night they did away with Ronald, it was no accident her heart was cut from inside her. They had tried to remove her as well. They had really tried to murder her. But she would remain visible. She would not take flight. She would continue to let her heart beat outside her body, hearing it gallop as she lay awake through each and every paralysed night, her new heart, her new husband, now her constant companion carried beside her, beating the message, I am alive, I have not stopped, I have defied them, and I want revenge.

God forgive her, but she did know about revenge, although one thing she didn't know was, where did the time go? Things she thought she'd believe forever, she kept forgetting. Did they play Abba's 'Super Trouper' on her wedding day, or did she hear it the evening – no, it was at night, late – they first met in the disco at Portrush? She was with a crowd of other teachers. This strapping fellow – not her immediate type, she'd hasten to add – he asked her to dance. That gentle Tyrone accent so complemented her own – didn't they make such sweet music, love took possession of them, they had to tie the knot. It was decided – as quick, as terrifying as that.

Still and all, she made him wait for the great pleasure. And the first night together it didn't hurt, it was lovely and he told her she was gorgeous – a pansy word, but perfect. That was as good a way as any of proposing. In fact she asked him. He refused. Can you believe it? It was on Valentine's Day and she had a perfect right to pop the question. He burst her balloon, saying he needed time. She laughed it off, insisting it was a joke. He didn't believe her. That was the worst thing about him. He never did believe her. And he wouldn't now if she were to walk into the living room where he was sprawled on a couch, watching ice skating, laughing at the men, spinning themselves silly, if she were to walk in and tell him there was a ferret in the garden.

But there it was. A ferret the colour of gold. It smelt of meat and wet clay. It was quite tame. It came into her hand and licked her face. She let it touch her fingers. It chewed on them gently, not so hard as to frighten her. Her flesh delighted in his taste. He started to move about her body, leaving her hand, clinging to her arm and going into her clothes, lying against her breast. She carried it into the house, going upstairs, resting on the bed as the ferret moved down her tits, between her legs and sucked her clean.

She did not call the police. She did not have to say, my husband is dead, my beautiful husband, and in his place, in my bed, there is a ferret. Please, come to my house and kill it. Shoot it dead. Blast its brains out. Take its neck and wring it. I want to hear its fucking bones crack. I want this ferret dead, for it has violated me, a poor widow, a woman it has tricked into trusting, because I might believe it to be an innocent animal. But it is not innocent. Nothing will ever be innocent again. If this creature survives, I will place it in a cage. I will never release it until it dies. I will never feed it. I will never let its soft lips touch water. I will never speak into its strange ears. I will keep it under lock and key forever. Key – I will throw away the key. It will never smell the light of day – it will die in its prison from thirst, starvation. Let it die of hunger, die of want. Let me watch it end its days and do nothing. This is the way I will prove I do not need rescuing from a ferret. Yes, I am a widow, I am alone. But I can still deal with this.

It was then the ferret found her throat. Its skin caressed her mouth. She patted her face, pointing to her mouth. He kissed her. She could feel the filth of its breath. She was going to be sick. But the ferret was now caressing her shoulder. She noticed the smell of drink, whiskey, brandy, it stank. The breath. But whose? His or hers? Before she could answer, the ferret raced from her bed. She did not scream. No fuss. It was all finished now. And who would believe her? They would think she was mad. Worse than mad, they would think her a pervert. She wondered if it was all a joke. A foul joke – blasphemous, a mockery of her mourning, a Protestant way of telling her, even in death, you are not fit to be one of us?

Perhaps that was why the following morning she was tempted to go to Holy Communion. Walk into the silent, damp church and have a feed of Christ. She did not believe in the body and blood of the Saviour, but if her husband could come back in the shape, the smell, the size of a ferret, then anything could happen. If she had taken Communion, it would have to be in the Catholic church in Coleraine. When she'd first arrived in the town, young and not giving a damn, this was how she'd ask for directions about this loyalist stronghold. Can you tell me where the hospital is – how far from the Catholic church? The hotel that serves tea on a Sunday when everywhere else is closed – that's right, the Lodge Hotel – is it near the Catholic Church? The locals might look at her with distaste. They might think she was dangerously bonkers. Still, they all knew where their enemy congregated. They told her exactly where it was located. That's what made her go there today, to get back her bearings, putting her hand in the holy, ice water font, feeling him where he was waiting in there, drenched, freezing her fingers, stopping her making the sign of the cross, his fur wet and soft, his teeth grinding into her. She was about to squeal, he was hurting her. About to let her rabid voice fill that hollow church. He was leaving her to bleed in that stagnant, blessed liquid. She did nothing. She just knew exactly what she was up against. She had to be rid of this animal.

The advertisement in *The Coleraine Chronicle* was simple. It read: Ferret found in garden. Good home required. She waited for replies. The answering machine delivered. She listened to them as she bathed, enjoying the strangers' voices filling the hall. The first woman said she was a sixty-seven-year-old grandmother. I have always wanted to cherish a ferret, please let me give it the good home required, she slurred on the phone. Country and western music played behind her, something about broken hearts and kings and queens. The old woman was joining in the song, forgetting she was still on the phone. Drunk as a skunk, the poor fool. Next was a farmer with a rough Antrim whisper of a voice. He had a grandson, a bit of a softie. I would like him to get an interest in ferrets. Toughen him up. If it bit, all the better. He needs to learn that life is not easy. My grandson. Jesus, who answers these advertisements? The last call was from a ferret farm away in the wilds of County Down. Should she wish to dispose of the creature, they would respect and rear it in an environment where it will thrive and learn to appreciate the ways of its own species. Our emphasis is on treating the beast as it should be treated. Go on, give in. Give us the ferret.

That was not possible. She found him dead this morning. Some of his golden hair lay in a puddle of blood. Who'd got him? A fox – a pair of hungry cats – or was it herself? The widow woman? Had she turned into a beast and could no longer be trusted? Should she be muzzled? Did she take the ferret by its neck in her mouth? Did she shake it till it howled for mercy? Did she swear, I will be revenged on the animal kingdom – I will tear this fucking house down – I will leave this town laid waste – I will bomb this cursed country – I will blow the bridge to bits. I will settle the score for my husband's death. My husband with no arms, no legs, no hands, no ring, no stomach, no face, nothing but a handful of golden hair in a puddle of blood, torn to ribbons, smashed in pieces, nothing left. Where has he gone to? My ferret, was that him? Could it be him? If you think so, then let me think so as well. Let me. Let me. Let me.

THE OPENING NIGHT

Once upon a time they sent flowers, bouquets to take the eye out of your head. Roses, carnations, wild cowslips and orchids, rarely lilies for they were deemed to be unlucky. Marvellous sweeps of every colour in the rainbow, waiting to be collected by all, from leading ladies down to the smallest walk-ons, making them feel special for the opening night. Nowadays, you could wander past the stage door, and it was like every other evening, not a bloom in sight. When did the habit cease? Was it gradual, or did it happen all of a sudden? Leo couldn't say for sure, but it was certain the youngsters didn't bother.

Maybe they were ignorant of the old ritual. Maybe, as they say about so much these days, they didn't give a living shit about such nonsense. It could well be that they actually knew nothing about the habits that were once so deeply ingrained, but surely they must have got wind of it somewhere along the line? He could guess, however, the most likely scenario. It could well be the case they just could not afford to send such luxury to people who were, in reality, strangers. Newcomers to the business had better things to spend their cash on.

So, had the old spirit of generosity vanished? The wonderful, reckless extravagance – gone down the toilet? Those splendid days when you might bankrupt yourself for the best part of a fortnight, splashing out your wages to put on a good show, just to let the world blaze with the news you'd arrived – loving the buzz, shake it out, baby, adding to its lavish sense of I'm me, and who's like me? Just who is like me?

They weren't all like that – actors. Some insisted, to anyone who'd listen, they were level-headed. They had to manage matters tightly, most of the money on offer was so lousy, what else could they do? He'd made mates with a fair few of that modest ilk. Most of them disappeared at the end of a run. It was rare to stay in permanent contact. The work scarcely allowed that intimacy. You're there, then you're not. Gone for ages, then they'd show their face again before the year was out, playing another part, always and ever complaining, the one thing that never changed. Complaining about the dough, about the director, about stage management. And complaining above all else that you know what – nobody ever listens. Why should we? Whingers they were, to a man and woman. But you could forgive that. You'd better. Hadn't you to work with them? And the best way to do that was let them rattle on, nod your head occasionally, and never contradict a word, no matter what baloney they talked.

Baloney it was, most of the time. He would be too polite to say so. If he had learned one thing from watching the ins and outs of manners on display when actors gather, then it was beyond a doubt clear in his head that they were all sensitive types. They might deny it. They would say a life of soul-destroying auditions, perfect for the roles they wanted, nearly but not quite getting them, that was when iron entered the soul. Jesus, did you need to be tough and grow a more-than-usually thick skin to survive. But that's when they were hiding what hurt them to the quick. That nearly getting things, but not quite. All the bravado they could muster would not match how deeply they'd been wounded, even the most successful. What had they to sacrifice to get where they are today? They'd paid an awful price, for it took their innocence. Gone, lost forever.

It was the easiest thing in the world to let this fact slip. A piece of cake to shatter them. You had to be on your permanent guard. One syllable might give it away that you saw signs they were ageing – less agile in how they covered the stage, their grace more of an effort, their robustness taking more out of them. Though they could be brutal in their manner with each other, no outsider – and we are all outsiders to that tribe – dared speak honestly. There are bad things associated with every job. Leo was sure of that, ask anybody, they'll say the same. The worst about his job – having to watch your mouth, seriously watch it, every time you spoke. At least he'd been well-trained in keeping secrets. Detta saw to that. She made a point of never letting Leo forget it.

She never let him forget much. There was a part of him that in a funny sort of way made him glad she behaved so. Hadn't she found him his first job? Gave him his start, as they say, and you should never forget what gratitude that debt placed on you. That trait ran through the veins of all belonging to the theatre. The biggest names might break down remembering old timers who'd been kind and welcoming to them years ago. One Hollywood star Leo had heard made a point of bringing a cup of tea to the oldest member of the company. This endeared her to all the players, but as it soon emerged that while the poor bitch might have star billing, she could not act on a stage, the consensus soon was would she not clear off it as soon as possible?

Detta was a cow of a different order, it pained him to say of his older sister. Leo would tell people he'd just fallen into this stage management thing, indeed this whole carry-on of theatre meant no more to him than the next man, to put folk at their ease when he was introduced in case they might be in a panic he was about to kiss them. Neither was true – that he would kiss them nor that he fell into this. Most people knew it was a lie. Detta berated him for his ignorance when he started. She implied he could barely read a script. That even writing down a prop list was beyond him. She kept him on his toes for a good reason. Her word had got him in, and if he was to be kicked out, it reflected badly on her. This was not permitted.

She let it be known to high and low Leo was employed in the theatre under false pretences. There was no other description for it. How else would he describe it? He was warned she could not provide for him all his and all her life. Remember that above all else the next time he thought he was too good to sweep a floor or wash a shirt that was needed for tonight's performance. She sincerely hoped he would never develop – as so many in his position do, getting their foot in the door because of who they knew – develop any uppity notions, for he deserved no better and no worse than what he was receiving.

No fear of him assuming airs and graces. She had instilled that he was so useless, each night he'd ask himself why didn't somebody knock at the stage door, asking for him by name? He would readily confess the game was up. If they didn't quite call the police, he should still hand himself in and claim any reward going for finding the guilty man behind this charade that was his whole incompetence.

But no one was brave enough – concerned enough – to spot the scale of his misdemeanours. He survived a sufficient time, not merely to be able to cover up his own mistakes, but the mistakes of others as well. Maybe – dare whisper this out of others' earshot – he was, yes, he'd say it, happy, living on the clippings of tin, struggling on this pittance of a wage, making ends meet, complaining like an actor.

That is what they taught him, by and large. Survival. Of course, he'd grown sharp enough to pick up a few other pointers. When your life is one long effort to see things through to the end of the week and not hear your guts rattle, you're glad of every little help. So Leo was learning how to make a pound go a long way, as was accurately observed of one well-dressed lady from the West of Ireland. It was widely wondered how does she afford the style? The same Miss Sligo never missed a bargain, I've seen her in action at the sales, a friend informed the assembly gathered after hours around a bottle of wine. She's like a jackal at a chicken carcass.

Through such manoeuvres he could sit for ages nursing his half of Guinness a whole night if necessary. It was taken for granted that the young ones would never be expected to stand a round. To their credit, no one encouraged that, so he was very rarely sucked into that ruinous system. There was a price to pay for being careful. He knew that for a few of the very hard drinkers he had been acquiring the reputation for being a tight arse, but better tight than hungry. Hadn't the example of his sister, Detta, served as a terrible warning how things can go belly-upward? At least no one could attach any blame on his head for this coming catastrophe. On that score he was innocent. And he should be. No one should point a finger in his direction for what was befalling there.

Of course there might well be dissenting voices to that opinion. What could Leo do about them? He was now old and ugly enough to know they all came from a clique that surrounded Detta, her coterie of pals, most of whom were as mad and, indeed, bad as herself, if truth be told. She had their sympathy, they let the world know, their hearts broke for her, they would do anything she asked, and look to where that sympathy had led her? Someone had to say this – a few declared they should have done so much earlier – but the plain truth was no company worth its salt would now touch Detta, not with a barge pole.

Hadn't she let down too many people in too many productions? All hands, friends as well as foes, had their horror stories to relate, so scarred by the experience that at the mention of the lady's name, some nervous souls cut the sign of the cross on themselves to ward off her evil presence, or at least to wish by the grace of God not to end where that one was heading. But she had long got away with her kamikaze tactics – how did someone not burst a blood vessel or throttle her, nobody could tell. One night in preview for Ibsen's *The Wild Duck*, she was said to start speaking gibberish, her defence being she was channelling the author, who wanted her to translate it back into the original Norwegian, of which she had not a word. She survived the boot on that occasion, and when normal service was resumed in English, gave a performance that suddenly, shockingly took the breath away for the sorrow of its secrets and how she sustained their telling. Miraculous, like her luck. It was just a question of how long it would last before it would run out. And it did run out. Luck always does.

He heard how it happened. Of course he had – how could he not? The dogs in the street knew. A whole production of Wilde's *The Importance of Being Earnest* was built around her. Fortunes were spent on set and costumes. Detta had already rejected all efforts to put herself as Lady Bracknell into any shape or form of a dress – no, this character was, in her way, transvestite, she would wear trousers, to hell with convention, it was there to be broken, what better man to prove that than Oscar himself? Rehearsals were reduced to screaming matches, the rest of the cast in tears, Detta, unmovable on this issue, stood on the floor intoning her lines like a Dalek, in particular killing stone dead any chance of a laugh Gwendolen, her daughter in the play, might provoke. She'll see sense, the company manager encouraged, she's trouble, but worth it. I don't think she is, the director ominously replied, I think she should be fired. Did she get wind of the threat? Last week of rehearsal, she was displaying signs of what she could do with this part. Why had she been cast in the first place. At the Saturday run-through, still refusing to be trussed up as some female sacrifice to the gods of Victorian propriety, that was when she delivered the works – her accent not so much cut glass as sheer diamond, her timing turning her fellow actors into her chorus, the assembled audience of front-of-house and ushers, box office and bar staff found themselves worshipping her, in a wonderful act of artistic subversion, making all and sundry as clever and witty as were she and the playwright, turning the cosmos into one joyous roar of laughter, moving as she did with such dexterity, dressed in ripped jeans, a T-shirt with Caravaggio on the front, poised in her bare, dirty feet. At the end of the morning, the applause was prolonged, kisses were exchanged, Detta would triumph – and we had once more survived the battle.

She walked. The morning of the first preview, she was gone. Out of the production. Disappeared. Thin air. No explanation. Not after the first day or week of rehearsal, but today, just before the first paying customers were due to arrive that evening, she had done a runner. This time she really did the dirty and left them in the lurch, just before the opening night, giving them next to no chance of getting anybody remotely ready or vaguely willing to cover her. Stay clear of this affair – it's bad luck, that was the general opinion. An aspiring actress – thirty years too young for the part – such were the dire straits of the company, she had to go on and read the lines cold. She didn't really help matters by saying that she understood why Detta might not want to wear Lady Bracknell's outfit, it didn't do her figure any favours either. The designer was heard to threaten he would be dug out of her if she had any more such comments to make about his clothes – have we got to the stage when any young pup can insult you if they felt like? You really should watch your mouth talking to me like that, the young one threatened, I'm doing you all a big favour going out in these forty shades of shite you call a dress, don't you forget it.

A fair few had to be held back from reaching for her after that. Send her out in her skin, the director hissed, maybe that might bring them in to see this fiasco.

Fiasco it was. The reputation of the show never recovered, and for the poor, cheeky brat, it proved to be her first and last part. A cruel business this, pity the kid, pity all involved, but pity had run out for Detta this time. There were signs, almost immediately, that the tide of good fortune had turned for her. Of course, she did her usual vanishing act, but now nobody tried their best to track her down, for it didn't matter if she showed her shameful face, looking to be forgiven once more, because who could want her back? Nobody wondered where her hiding place would prove to be on this occasion. Let her rot in it. Leo alone, her brother, was making frantic phone calls, and scurrying best as he could to the usual haunts, bars where the roughest of the rough thought twice about using the gents. No joy. Her agent knew nothing, and didn't want to know. Beyond help, that was the verdict.

He feared for Detta's sanity – he feared for her life if she should discover how all hands were being washed clean of her and her doings. People, Leo felt, who should have given a damn, they didn't. Maybe the profession was changing, getting harder or something, and Detta hadn't noticed. There seemed no desire to indulge her any longer. She herself had brought this on, let her deal with it, but never again was good money going to be wasted trusting she would do the decent things eventually and honour the contract she'd been paid to finish. No one cares if I live or die, not one, you included, she ranted against Leo when she finally switched on her phone and rang from a fancy hotel in Adare where she'd once read they did a cheap deal for future brides-to-be and their mothers. Not even they had fallen for the line she was peddling - so traumatised by her daughter's death, she now was in such deep denial she'd invented a wedding. The management smelt a rat when it became clear that in her trauma she might expect them to waive the whole bill.

When this escapade got out, the consensus was, Christ, could you be up to that witch? But her smartness softened no hearts, as it might have before. It just made her more of a pathetic laughing stock. Not that she allowed herself to listen, too busy as she was screeching to any who'd heed her. I've given this filthy profession, this city – this country – at home and abroad, so much through the best years of my life. What's my thanks? It's a quick fuck off, Detta. Deal with your depression on your own. Isn't that so, Leo? she accused her brother. Well, I'm glad I did let them down if they say I did. Cock-a-hoop, as our dead mother would describe herself, before one of her attacks, taking leave of her senses and only I could bring her back. Do you remember those sessions, dear brother? What did you do? Nothing, like the rest of them. Well, I'm happy I've let the whole circus – the whole shebang of them – let them down. Isn't that what they've been doing to me since the unfortunate day and hour I chanced my bad luck and set foot on a stage? How many of you fuckers have I carried on my shoulders – you included, Leo? Too many – far too many – that's how they have worn me to the bone and brought me to the end of my tether.

That was the bold Detta's reading of her story, and Leo, for one, certainly knew his sister well enough to be sure she would be sticking to it. She sounded so convincing blaming everybody else for her misfortune. But then if she was one thing above all else, it was convincing. Since she was a toddler, he was told, the same lady could get the world in all its teeming multitudes to credit every word out of her mouth as gospel truth, even if a titter of wit, an iota of common sense itself, ruled it impossible. Why was she so readily believed? Uncles, aunts, all belonging to them, they were falling over themselves to be charmed by her. Could it be the very sound of her voice, its lilt? Was it the way she could imagine what should have happened, rather than what did? How her eyes bored into your brain, daring you to point the finger, accusing her, she was telling tall, tall tales? This dangerous habit stuck. It became her way of life. She earned her bread and butter defying the facts. Why bother to check them? What you say to people goes in one ear and out the other. That was her philosophy. Everybody eventually forgets everything. And forgives.

But this latest no-show, that was most emphatically not going to be forgiven. It made the papers. Not the front pages, but the arts section where the theatre second-string critic felt it a moral duty to list in chronological order how often she'd missed performances. He even questioned the long-standing rumour she'd fired herself from a seriously big movie because she refused to do a nude scene. That story always went before her. She neither confirmed nor verified it. Let people talk. Now, it was implied maybe it was not a rush of modesty that won the day back then but the need for a long lie-in. More than a few read this and put a thumb to their nostril, sniffing. This was serious stuff indeed. The whole fad for cocaine was long over. No-one now would dare supply a line, let alone the profusion that once wafted by you when the world knew where you could get your hands on whatever you liked. Those days were gone, and Detta soon felt she too was a goner with them.

That dawned on her a lot sooner than Leo had imagined it would. The first big, bad sign was when one of the fellow cast members of the Wilde play cut her dead in the local theatre restaurant. Why in hell had she ventured in there alone? Did she still think she had the brass neck to carry that off solo? And the waiters – she'd tipped them well over the years – what was their beef with her? Why did they seem to be a lot more subdued tonight? Whose corns had she trod on there? She was dining solo – of course they found her a table, but the welcome was not – how you say in these parts – it was not warm. Is this a wake I've stumbled into or something? she mocked when she failed to raise any sort of smile in the room. Am I being refused at the rails? Again she listened to herself using one of their mother's expressions, but no one rose to her bait nor remarked on how long it had been since they'd heard that old chestnut.

Not a being joined her at her solitary table. Familiar faces steadfastly avoided glancing at her. Should she brazen it out? Walk up to where they sat, plonk herself down, and just converse as if nothing had happened? But it had, and to her shock, she wasn't exactly sure what. She was left to eat her meal. Chew the steak, tough as cement, carved into meticulous bloody fragments. Swallow, with great effort, spinach drowning helplessly in cream. Ignore the raw, revolting chips, white as the plate beneath them. Only the manager, handsome, welcoming as ever, had any words with her. She loved him but could not bear his kindness this evening. There was no need to avail of the late opening hours tonight in the restaurant. She was in a taxi home before half past ten.

She made her exit, and no one stood up for her. That's what she reported to Leo, letting him in on the news she was now persona non grata in the old haunt. He could tell from the tremor in her voice on the message she left for him, this carry-on had shaken her. She started for some reason to tell him the favourite Mrs Patrick Campbell story, how she demanded a cab take her to Piccadilly Circus, but the driver refused, claiming the mutt she constantly carried in her arms would piss everywhere. Nonsense, she stormed, and the cab wafted down Shaftesbury Avenue. When she got out and paid, he looked and saw a large puddle of water on the seat. He roared in a voice all London could hear, Oy Missus, I knew it, your dog peed in my taxi. No, the grande dame thundered back, *I* peed in your taxi. Detta cackled, to reassure him she was in command of this and every situation. Ring her back soon. He would do so tomorrow. He must remember that. There was no necessity just yet. Then, a thing unheard of – she rang him before nine o'clock in the morning. Jesus, she must be really panicking. This was deep shit all right, and she knew she was in it. Of course, she left no message this time. Only the command. Ring back.

He didn't.

He was shocked at what pleasure that silence brought. But he would phone – in a few hours. First thing then. If he were to call too early, there was every chance she'd hurl a mountain of abuse at him for not realising normal people aren't like himself. When they have to get up with the lark, they might go back to bed for a few hours' more kip. She wasn't in dreamland this morning though. Her number came up again, this time leaving no message. He relented and rang her.

She asked him was he thick in the head? Did he not know she needed to talk? He said he did have some awareness that was the case. Why else would he be on the bloody blower to her? She informed her brother that she did not like his tone. Just who in hell did he think he was? Who do you imagine you are talking to? It would be hard not to know who you are, very hard, he dared answer her. Listen to me, you ungrateful bastard, Detta was barking now, I got you every bit of work you've ever skived your way through, I saw to it you were kept in a job when every management didn't so much want rid of you as put you down in such a fashion you'd never darken their door ever again. Who was it had it in her to put the fear of God into them, not to give you such a root up the arse you could taste your own spleen? If you were never fired, there was one reason for that, and only one. Me – you do realise that. Don't you ever forget one fact. I can see to it very soon you never work in a theatre in this town again. Do you understand?

Fuck me, how many times had she threatened that before? He'd lost count. It was now a standing joke. The ridiculous wagon threw this in his face, as she had with every other maggot – yes, she called them maggot – who'd dare disobey her commands. Some pitied her, some laughed at her, most just ignored her and the like, living in a world where such commands had no meaning – no power – for the theatre as she knew it did not exist anymore. Blasted it was, blown away by the wind. No one survived, not a being, who took their bearings from a world time forgot. Doing what you're told had been removed from the virtues any enterprising girl or boy paid the slightest attention to in their climb up the ladder of how to succeed in show business without really trying. Who heeded such niceties these days? Who you knew didn't matter anymore. And if you believed that, it was safe to assume you believed anything.

He switched off his mobile, before he said what he wanted – what Detta deserved to hear. I'll be earning a wage for a lot longer than you now will, best beloved. He didn't come out with it as savagely as he should have, once again he bit his tongue, yet that is what hit him hard. How in Christ's name would a woman addicted to burning the banknotes – how would this fucker, his could-be-gentle, always generous sister Detta survive? What in hell was going to happen there? Of course she was good – among the very best going – and she got buckets of offers. The bucket was emptying. Yes, she had made money, serious money. She'd spent it like water, pouring through her hands. What did she own? A cottage in Chapelizod, and she had to pay off her useless lover Mark to get rid of him from the house. That's all it amounted to in terms of what belongings Detta had to show for her years of slogging. Did she ever save a penny? That he doubted. All right, she had helped buy his tiny flat in the Liberties. She had been kind enough to put down a deposit for him after scoring some cash from the BBC in the days when they did pay actors well for doing decent work – and she had been more than good as Mary Crawford in an excellent *Mansfield Park*. Though the book itself she dismissed as cat's piss and she personally would have dismembered Fanny Price, the manipulative little wagon of a heroine. So, she'd handed over what their father would have called a dig-out, purchasing a home for himself. Through his own efforts he was paying his mortgage, as was only right and proper. Now, up shit creek, how did she think she was going to manage? Dine on fresh air, drink only tap water, heat herself by blowing air through her fingers? He could not keep her.

But for all the insanity past and present, for all the bonkers behaviour, she would not have called on him for support. Ask her best friend – maybe her only friend – the hairdresser Rose Lynch, for confirmation. Rose swore that Detta, despite her lack of sense, the Detta she knew would never go entirely over the edge. Some hand – call it whose you like, God, Detta's father and mother, her guardian angel, if that's your fancy – this almighty power had held her back and stopped her smashing her life into bits, though there had been many a close shave. The same Rose knew of what she spoke when she sighed they had been in some scrapes together. Rose had also not done too badly with her own adventures. Rumour had it she'd spent six months in a Greek jail, nearly as bad as a Greek hospital, she quipped, and she implied if the subject reared its ugly head, she was a lucky lady not to still be banged up there – something to do with forged travellers' cheques or drugs or some such nonsense, who remembers? Hard to place the now always immaculately groomed Rose snivelling, terrified behind bars, facing a daily hiding from anyone who looked at her, but that was the story. She'd got through it, and she was always convinced her great mate, Detta, the only one brave and good enough to visit her so far away – it could bring tears to Rose's eyes thinking of it – Detta would step back at the last minute, and save herself. More than that, she would put in a spectacular comeback. She'd done it before – would do it again, would always do it.

Then why was Rose Lynch knocking at his door, asking

if he'd found Detta? Did he know she'd called round to Rose very late last night? She was asking – begging for her head to be shaved entirely. Her cheek was bleeding. Why was it? No answer but a fit of crying. Rose took her in, fetched hot water and wiped her clean as best she could, refusing point blank to bald her. That gorgeous red hair – what could Detta be thinking? And Detta then said something exceedingly odd.

She asked Rose, can you tell me my name? I think I've forgotten it. Rose would not now and never would tolerate Detta's silly games. Straight out she told her where to get off. So you won't help me to find out, is that the case? Detta challenged. And there's when she burst into floods of tears that wouldn't stop, no matter what persuasion Rose tried to stem the waterworks. Her life was an awful mess, Detta was bawling. It always is, it always has been, you silly bitch, Rose in her best, most normal way tried to reassure, hoping both of them might soon stumble on the ludicrous side to all this and start guffawing at the right pair of eejits they made. That wasn't going to work this time.

I can't remember my name – I really can't, Detta kept repeating, until Rose was tempted to slap her hard. She kept firm hold on her temper because experience taught her blowing a fuse would only increase the hysterics, and nobody wanted that. I'm losing a grip, I can't remember lines, faces, moves – and now, it's my name, Jesus, what is my name? What am I going to do? Detta was whimpering, and for a split second, Rose believed her. Now she had to ask Leo had he witnessed any signs of this before? No, he hadn't. Did it run in the family, strains of the dreaded disease? No, he lied – Rose might be a bosom buddy to his sister, but she and all her like were as good as strangers to him, they'd never made him welcome, so there was not a hope he would exchange very private details about his flesh and blood to this one, standing there as good as mocking the plight of poor Detta. Rose would surely find our mother's mad antics in her dotage a pantomime to hurl abuse at when the chance to do so next presented itself. Now she was feigning concern, asking what they were going to do about it.

He didn't know. You don't know – that's all you can offer? she threatened him. It was, yes. Do you know what you are? You are a useless bugger, she condemned him, utterly, utterly useless. But on this occasion, she was short of the backing her usual cohort, Detta, would provide, their two voices united against him, blaming him for whatever mishaps he had brought upon himself, not giving the respect he'd merited for enduring them, running him down constantly. He looked straight at Rose. He might well be useless, he'd venture to say, but he still managed to hold down a steady job. He was trusted to be what he was, one of the best stage managers going, though he said it himself. And he needed to be in rehearsals soon, so if Rose would excuse him, he'd bid her a good morning.

That was it then? Was he not going to head out with her this instant to Chapelizod? If Detta should not be found there, would he not help search for her? He wouldn't. He had fucking enough. That sister of his was ruined – spoilt rotten by all unfortunate enough to be held ransom by her. She had finally – finally driven him well beyond the absolute end of what he would tolerate. He was going to be where he should be – where she should be – at work. And do what? Rose challenged him. Run and fetch tables and chairs, cups and saucers? Make little scribbles in his copy book to remind actors where they'd wandered during the last run? That was all he was fit for. Was he even up to that? Didn't a woman director brought from England threaten to have him fired, his nervousness annoyed her that much? Everybody knew that. Detta consistently talked people into keeping him on when he was starting as assistant stage manager.

Everybody needs to learn the ropes at the beginning, he defended himself. The only rope you should be learning is the one to tie around your sorry neck, she dismissed him. Had he no consideration for the sister who, if truth be told, actually kept him from the gutter? That is where I'll land you, he warned, if you continue this abuse – how dare you talk to me like that. Because you deserve no better, Rose reminded him, you are not fit to tie your

117

sister's shoes. With that she shot him a look that told him she knew.

It was not the worst of secrets. Nor was it dirty or shameful. He always wore slip-ons because he'd never managed the knack of knotting his laces. Some crime to admit, but he knew from the way Rose Lynch hurled this at him clearly here was information that had provided a massive burst of glee from time to time for the pair of her and Detta. It could be construed as a very black mark against him – weren't stage managers supposed to be practical people? By and large they were, and at this point of his career he would include himself among the best of them, yet that one manoeuvre was beyond his skills, leaving him all fingers and thumbs and none of them working together. It was strictly his business, and he preferred to keep it so. Naturally, that didn't stop Detta announcing how Leo was humiliated in school when a teacher told him in front of the class to tie his lace and the poor little fool couldn't. She had no pity for him then, but she did when Ma, in one of her crazy moods, went to cane him after she heard he'd shamed the family in the classroom. Detta caught the rod, bearing the brunt of its lash herself, broke it using all her strength, telling their mother she would no longer put up with this cruelty, nor would Leo. He loved her for doing so, but wanted to choke her when she broadcast why his choice of footwear was seriously restricted. When that humour hit her, she'd go further and declare she considered it a miracle he'd learned to clean his own arse. There may come a time you'll be expecting me to clean yours, he mocked back, don't push your luck. For some reason, it shut her big mouth.

Now here he was listening to stories that she could not remember her name. That she wanted to shave off her crowning glory. This was beyond the usual daftness during and after a binge. Sure as eggs are eggs, his sister Detta would trump a session on the tear with some act of remorse that would silence all accusation pitted against her, spending every red cent she possessed if that were necessary. She kissed your husband – or she kissed your wife – with such passionate force they might be gasping for breath. She claimed Robert Mitchum taught her that lesson in love, and he might well have, since she always declared men no longer kiss like Robert Mitchum. Inevitably tongues were wagging. The following morning, two flexi-tickets to fly to the States, any airport east or west coast, they might pop through your post box, the covering note reading only DXX. She spilt red wine on your carpet, emptied a box of Saxa salt into it and made the stain worse. You'd soon be holding in your hot hand a voucher for Peter Linden's in Blackrock, the best Persian rug shop in Dublin. Maybe she ripped down your new drapes from the windows because that day the colour brown annoyed her intensely – she could not bear to be subjected to this ugliness a second longer. Then she would immediately send a cheque for a sum of money far more than the curtains could possibly be worth on the strict condition you should cash it and buy another pair, or else she would come round and vomit profusely on the originals if they were rehung in any quarter of the house, including the attic. For all this exceedingly expensive carry-on she was renowned, loved even, and feared sometimes. Christ, what could happen if that woman accepted your invitation to go anywhere? What would enter her head was never predictable. From what he deciphered of her present shenanigans, just at this minute Leo did not know what was possessing her, nor could he guess.

But he would still not give her the satisfaction of ringing her again to see was she all right. And he kept his mobile switched off going into the rehearsal room. From the looks he was not given – every one of the team, from the most esteemed director down to the youngest bit-part, studiously, simultaneously avoided his eye, so he knew they must know all, or as damned near to all that it made no difference. Still, they would get no joy out of him.

If they thought he was going to let out a diatribe against his sister, they would be disappointed. Should they be expecting him to offer excuses for Detta, they could be waiting till Christmas. And if they imagined for a minute they were going to hear what distressed him most about this particular episode, then he could not oblige them, since he had no clear notion of what it was exactly he should be terrified against, although something was stirring from deep in his brain that he dreaded above all else. He knew that Detta let the world in on the information that savage drinking habits were a curse on their family. Why could she not have sealed her mouth shut? She made such a song and dance of what they'd endured as children watching both their parents drown their sorrows until she was blue in the face cursing the bastards. Leo wanted to go under the table and not emerge until she had exhausted what seemed some nights like a subject that would never let her give up the ghost. All right, a touch of excess was in their blood, but had she not coped with it perfectly before?

No, not perfectly, not recently. She had slipped up very publicly, very badly. She'd managed to convince a big-time director she befriended when he was starting out in BBC Northern Ireland she would make ideal casting as a mother grieving for her child taken from her by nuns. This guy had gone on to achieve great things. He could have had his pick of British or American names. He chose Detta. She repaid him by referring to the picture as yet another *Where's my Babba? Give Me Back My Babba* film, so beloved by the English dramatising recent Irish history. She knew this director's first wife and contacted her to say they should get together again, despite their prolonged, painful custody battle that was still on-going.

For the sake of old times, the poor man could put up with much, but every morning she would appear looking absolutely wretched, so it was certain her role would be cut to ribbons. Better to bite the bullet and fire her, which he did. So now he was useless, the other actors assholes, and her agent was fit to be tied in rage, threatening to do as he should have done years ago and remove her from his books. Let him – she laughed it off, mumbling to herself about water and ducks' backs. Nothing rumbled her, she maintained.

But strains were showing. A few hotels were refusing to serve her at the bar. The old trick of getting one over on them by booking a room and ordering from there – that was now off the agenda. She just could not afford such messing, and at last that had hit home. That much she knew. Never let the lousers grind you down – that was always my motto, Detta would fanfare. Perhaps she had started to grind herself down. The warning signs were obvious, screamingly so, but who was there to admit they could hear screaming? All of this trepidation was crowding his mind, but Leo gave no sign of the panic that he was feeling. Not a chance he would blubber. This morning he prided himself that he was working better than he'd ever done before – anticipating what the director would want as clearly as if Leo were a mind reader, watching the actors like hawks, sensing when they were going to make the slightest mistake in the lines, whispering the correct version, not annoying them in the smallest way, nobody throwing a tetchy 'I know' when he spoke to remind them of their error.

Maybe they were just being courteous to him because of the circumstances. They did believe he was dependent on Detta. How she was the only one belonging to him. How he did need her to ask how was he getting along, for she alone wanted to know. And she could be lying cold in a ditch somewhere – he had no idea. It was a terrible thing he had done to her. Neglected her last night. Abandoning her this morning, as if she meant nothing to him. Letting that interfering bitch Rose Lynch listen to him running his sister down. Jesus, she must have enjoyed that, high and mighty, know-it-all Miss Lynch, hearing his nearest and dearest rip themselves apart. Why had he done it? He was about to excuse himself from the rehearsal. Tell no lies – say he needed to make an urgent phone call, let it cause whatever comment it caused.

But there was no need to interrupt – Rose Lynch did that for him. What was she doing standing there while the rehearsals continued? Did she not know that nobody, but nobody, entered there, unless invited? And why was she shouting at him, get down to the foyer – for Christ's sake. He got down the stairs, not bothering with the lift. Not noticing if Rose were following him. Just hell-bent on finding out what Detta – what in hell was she doing?

He got there to see his sister squatting naked from the

waist down. A patch of piss soiled about her ankles. Silent as the grave, she ignored all eyes watching, women, men, most of them in tears. I don't know where I am, Detta told her brother, is it the ladies' toilet? What are men doing in the ladies' toilet?

Rose it was went over to help her dress again, keeping on and on whispering, we're here, we'll mind you, we're here. But who am I? Detta wanted to know, who are you? And why is that fellow watching me? Detta, it's me, your only brother, Leo told her. Have you come to see me? she asked. I have, he answered. Why – is this the opening night? Why are there no flowers? She demanded. I took them with me, they're already at home, he fibbed. You should not have done that, she declared, it might be unlucky for the run. Who was it thought that? Which of the old actors? I can't remember – can you? No, I can't, he admitted truthfully, but come with me and we'll rack our brains, we'll cast our minds back, we'll find the answer, you and me together, will you come with me?

Will you be good to me? she asked her brother. Yes, he answered, and he meant it. He really did, Christ help her, and Christ help him as well.

ANIMALS

Years ago, centuries ago, since this happened. Still and all, I walk fast if I ever find myself back in Ranelagh, then a warren of digs and flats, myself in a single bedsitter sharing a bath, a toilet, cooking for myself alone on a single gas ring and grill, as we all did in those long departed, desperate days. Yes, I got out of that place, that time, and would I ever return, in dreams, in nightmares? No – never, no.

We trained together. Not for soccer, nor Gaelic football, and no man from our corners of the country would touch rugby. Even watching that game when we were in our prime was a big deal in certain quarters, seeing it was maintained that only wealthy louts disfigured themselves legally on the blood-soaked pitches. For that reason people should not encourage them by watching. When I see pubs packed now, all eyes mesmerised, every try and penalty cheered to the rafters, a nation united, I think these are changed times, changed utterly, and remember how it stood once, not that long ago.

But who am I to preach? I was never that greedy for playing team sports. Sure, as a school boy, we were all threatened, like it or lump it, to get togged out. Like most, I did as instructed, but it might be more than fair to say my heart was never exactly in it. It was not that I disliked the near nakedness of others so close to my own. More that I did not trust it. But I had, at least, to pretend I had a passion for some sort of game. I was lacking in the courage to risk the ridicule of admitting I preferred tennis, so as soon as I was free to leave the pitch behind me, I did. I chose athletics, much more my cup of cyanide.

Fair to say, I shattered no records, local or otherwise, so I was not under any illusions our club would select me for a championship. But I kept it up, I took pleasure in staying fit enough to push myself beyond a few miles for a strenuous trek in wind, rain or shine. It cleared my brain, such exercise. My mind went blank of its own accord, allowing me to obliterate the wars and wrongs that did accumulate about me in the school room. And I would have been more than content to keep stretching myself as far as possible on my own, if he had not inquired would I like company when I was running? How could I say no? Was there anything about him that might deserve such an unmannerly refusal? Nothing I could notice, or for that matter, nothing anyone else would, I'd wager. Matthew was one of our best teachers – that was agreed, no word against him. Strict in the class, but popular with his peers when he was, like myself, starting out in his career. A civil fellow, strongly built, respected by staff and students alike, though the word soon spread the boys feared him. And he did demand they do more homework than the rest of us young schoolmasters might.

He expected that work to be properly done and digested, ready for presentation the following day. The consequence was him getting his pupils great exam results already. Parents were urging their children to be in his class. He seemed set on a glorious career, the future beckoning him into becoming maybe the youngest ever head teacher Ireland ever anointed. I choose that word with care, and I mean it. Back then there really was a sort of aura around teaching. It's gone and good riddance to it. But these were the murmurings behind his back, sometimes sufficiently audible to ensure he'd catch a word here and there. Should things come to pass as they were being foretold, maybe he might remember old friends when he basked in power.

Such was his popularity, none could begrudge him these good wishes. He was smart enough never to speak up about his ambitions, if he had any. Only one rumour darkened the bright horizon. This was that he'd been particularly severe on one chap, smaller than the rest of his year's intake. The boy could use size and a pretty smile to get himself out of every trouble. Not with the brave Matthew O'Loughlin he couldn't. Whatever happened, the little fellow must have felt genuine fear, for he did the unthinkable in a boys' school. He cried. Blubbed in fact, quivering, snot in his nose – the works.

That was said to have inflamed O'Loughlin. Such snivelling he absolutely could not abide, and he would not stand for it under any circumstances. He started to call the child names, and to encourage the other boys to follow suit. Somehow, he reined himself in, containing his ire, and he left the class of lads to recover their nerve while he went to have a smoke in the teachers' toilets. The nicotine calmed him down enough to let him return and finish the lesson.

The runt that he mocked, he was still sobbing. O'Loughlin changed his attitude to him entirely. He patted him on the head. He gave him his handkerchief to dry his eyes and blow his nose. He told the rest of the youngsters sometimes it was a manly thing to weep. There had been a programme recently – a history programme about the First World War where old soldiers cried for their comrades killed as boys not much older than you are now. They did the right thing, mourning their fallen friends. So no mocking, was that understood?

Nothing would be known of this if he had not been spotted having the cigarette when he should be inside teaching. There could be only one man who was acting the spymaster. No surprises here whatsoever – Fergus

Lipton, the bastard head of mathematics caught him in the act. Well, he spotted him through the open door, and that sighting was sufficient. Why was Lipton such a shit? It was said his middle names were Francis Xavier, hence his nickname Madame X, or even Lana Turner who starred in the picture of that name. Only the boldest of the bold dared use either insult, even behind his back. Still and all, Lipton knew what was thought of him, and I believed he had lost the head a bit, wanting revenge against the world, or in this specific case, against the handsome O'Loughlin.

Lipton interrogated some stragglers leaving school later that evening. They gave him all he needed to know. Once he had got full wind of events, learned their chapter and verse as he himself described the incident, well, he was shocked, very shocked. He had to do the right thing about this — he really had to. So he let all and sundry in on the knowledge that Mr O'Loughlin as good as lost the rag entirely before the juniors in Year Two. Not good — not good at all, in Lipton's opinion, the head should hear of it, but not from him. No one could accuse him that he was one to carry stories and get someone, innocent or even guilty, into hot water. That was his way of making sure the story was brought exactly where he'd intended it to be. Christ curse him and all who speak when they should be silent, let them learn to shut their mouths.

Still and all, though, Matthew was shitting bricks. He made no secret about the state he was in, much to Lipton's great pleasure, cackling with joy as he observed that O'Loughlin's mother might be saying an extra decade of the rosary for her fine lump of a son. Still, the old brute was thwarted. Our boss was a fair man who weighed things up evenly. He could settle this kerfuffle without too much incident. He did the opposite of what Lipton wanted. Instead, Matthew was praised for doing good work, indeed excellent work with last year's Leaving Cert class in French. There was a first time for everything in any school, and this was such an occasion, when every boy managed at least to scrape a pass, even in the compulsory oral. Now that was such an achievement – a very tall order indeed as it was the devil's own task to get lads even to assume an accent that might with some charity be described as credible. O'Loughlin himself was such a strapping bucko that they took him seriously when he insisted on conducting the lesson in the foreign language, of which he had excellent command. Hearing his fluency, they lost all fear of being called – what would they have been called? Soft, I suppose.

Was I soft to tell him I was entirely on his side in the whole ridiculous affair? That Lipton was a prize pig for squealing the way he did? That I wondered why he had done it? Jealousy, boredom, just for the fun of it maybe? Who could tell? O'Loughlin told me he'd rather not know the reasons behind such dirty treachery, for treachery it was to turn against your own, and though he was not long in the profession, he still considered loyalty to be a virtue. But what's done was done, it was now buried, done with, and the problem was no longer his. He would as well put it out of his head as remember. Would I not agree?

He did say he was grateful – immensely so – for the support. It meant much to him, we must sit and have a drink as a thank you. I let him know that this would be grand by me. My very words exactly, no more, no less, no encouragement of any sort apart from that simple statement. But he must have picked up there was more than I'd intended, or even imagined. Maybe he was just a pushy git, because it was then he asked me was I still at the running? Wasn't I great the way I kept it up so dutifully? He reported he often saw me pounding my way about the town's pavements in drenching rain or round the school's playing fields, letting nothing ever distract me. Often he was on the verge of shouting well done, man – keep it up. Something to encourage me onward. But he didn't like to interrupt my concentration, even if it might bring my lovely smile to my serious face. My lovely what? I asked in shock, but I got no repeat of the compliment. No, rather he asked out straight would I do him a favour. Has it anything to do with my lovely smile, because if it does, mister, you can forget— He interrupted, would I mind if from time to time he might join me and we could run in unison?

He thought he could keep pace with me from what he

saw, so he wouldn't slow me down. He had loved running in his PE class as a teenager. They had a brilliant coach who ran for Ireland in the four hundred metres. That was his favourite distance, wasn't it mine? How could he guess that was the case? Just a feeling, put it down to a hunch. And he was more than willing to let me dictate how we would proceed – if he trailed after, then dump him. But was he being too forward – did he overstep the mark requesting this?

What could I say? No chance I'd refuse. Did he read something into that? How would he? Was I too quick to say – yes, that's grand, absolutely grand. Nothing better than a bit of company. No, I was anything but offended. What made him think I would be? People get very touchy these days, over the slightest things, he explained, I never like to stir shit or to give the wrong idea, so I make sure everything is all right. Come along anytime, I interrupted, tired of his apologising, for which there was no need. In good weather I run after school – in the late afternoon. Would that suit? To a T, he smiled, to a T.

That was how we began, not so much to pal about together – more just spending an evening once in a while in the pub. I would never describe it as my local. To this day, I've never had such a watering hole. No need for it. I drink – I drank less – a lot less than himself. I still was not sure why he was hanging around with me. The man, to my best knowledge, had a fair few girlfriends on the go at the same time. They did take up most of his time. None seemed to hang around too long, taking into account the variety of names he was always rushing off to meet. Very rarely one would be brought along to meet me. It seldom occurred, and I was grateful for that. The women themselves seemed even more uncomfortable than I was to be there, playing bloody gooseberry, so I soon made my exit after standing my round – let no one accuse me of being miserly. He was as glad as I was I'd done a runner, so why in hell's name had he invited me in the first place?

He really never let me in on that secret, but I do have to say that there was one time he seemed disappointed at my going – sufficiently so to insult the young one, maybe not too seriously. Enough though to distress us both a little, me and her. He used the word fucker with such venom and it clearly shocked her. She let it pass, as I did, for I felt it was directed at her. Then within a few minutes, he said it again, she very definitely was his target of abuse. Sorry, he excused himself, what am I saying? I should bite my tongue. I'm upsetting Louise with my bad language. She won't speak to me all evening now, but then, you weren't saying a lot before, were you?

It wasn't much of an apology, you might say. He laughed as he put his hand on her knee and rubbed it harshly. She startled. I was deeply embarrassed for her, and yet I knew there was only one thing to be done. Gulp down the last of my Guinness, even if it choked me – and it nearly did so – be out of there as rapidly as possible and leave them to their devices, none of my business, thank you very much, but I'm clear of here.

Are you rushing off? Don't, he ordered, Louise doesn't want you to leave, and neither does myself. Stay, give us a bit more of your craic he demanded, and I realised this was more of a threat than anything else. No, I'll just be going, I insisted. Are you driving by any chance past my flat? she wondered. If you are, I'll take a lift. She won't – you won't, he instructed her, and I saw her turn puce with shock. You stay here till I decide we leave, have you got that? His quiet voice left her in no doubt he meant what he said. So she nodded. I turned on my heel and departed, not getting caught up in this row.

Next time we were running, he matched me step by step. Any chance I might have had to lose him a little or race past him for five minutes at least – not a big deal before this – he would not relent, keeping exact pace. I thought, stupidly enough, this might be that he could offer some explanation for behaving like such a brute, but none came, not a sausage. In fact, if truth were to be told, I'd never remembered him so quiet. Did he say a word other than to suggest a quick pint? Back in the same bar he sat there more subdued than I'd ever seen him. Why then did he start to talk about where he came from?

It was some backwater in the midlands of Ireland, the

godforsaken midlands, a town I'd never been to – never heard of until I met him and never wanted to hear about after he left my life. As he spoke, he seemed to be summoning strange spirits out from somewhere, for his voice was as quiet as it had been aggressive the other time, swearing himself stupid, threatening his innocent girl. His accent deepened, as if he'd never spent a day or night away from where he was born. I had to struggle to make out precisely what he was trying to say. I'm not suggesting he started out by admitting he was ashamed of his town, but you might have thought so from how he didn't seem to want anyone else to get wind or word of what he thought about home.

First he got stuck into how tough it was to do at all well in his school, where nobody had any intention of getting to university. If they entertained such a dream, it would soon be kicked out of them by their elders and betters, or by the other boys passing their time before they were guaranteed a job in the meat factory. He said each and every one of the lads, himself definitely included, could impersonate the many sounds a condemned pig made on its way to the knife. I begged him not to demonstrate in any shape or form, and he obliged, keeping silent on the subject. It was nearly a miracle he'd managed to get the necessary honours grade for a scholarship to college, but he put his head down and worked, as he had to, like the devil, to beat the bastards of teachers and shopkeepers that would hold the likes of himself and myself down. The low voice had vanished. It was now shrill as a whistle, and I shot him a look of warning to bring it down, the volume. His answer was to order instantly more pints, though I was not in the mood for another and had not swallowed the best part of my first one.

I was now truly on my guard in the light of how this performance was developing, but he was on his best behaviour. Like a lamb, you might say, an angry lamb, but a manageable one. He asked me why was I not drinking, seeing me nurse an untouched Guinness. I told him he knew I was sparing with the alcohol, so don't mind me. Had he inquired, I would have refused a second one, but he didn't, so, no hard feelings. If he fancied more, have it – I'd sit it out with him while he finished it.

He shook his head – he knew when enough was as good as a feast, he would be like myself, a good boy. Still, that did not stop him talking. Telling how watchful he'd had to be all his childhood – all his adult life. How he needed to keep a serious grip on the booze. No let-up there, never could be. How he was very particular about the friends he could trust to go on the tear with. His da was an old soak – a drunken bastard, another one in the long annals of fuckable Irish fathers whose wives lived in terror of them. And the kids, they all did too, especially the small ones.

He could scare the wits out of all his brood. They should

be scared. More than one night, late coming home, he vomited all over the cot where his latest young infant was lying, leaving the whole house stinking and in uproar, the mother screaming he was a skunk and a complete swine, a swine. The father thought this hysterically funny, grunting – grunting – grunting, then asking the unfortunate woman, would you leave me if you could, you fucker? I'd kill you, if I could, she informed him, roaring. Then why don't you – why don't you put me out of my misery? he demanded of her.

She didn't, naturally. They were still hitched together. Still living as one, in the same nowhere, up the main street, down the same street, in the middle of this island of Ireland, where no one arrived, no one left. He hated with all his being – he hated going home. Hated the pong of the place. Hated crowding round the table like dogs round a dish on the floor. Hated having to share a single bed, squeezing the whole size of himself, a fully grown excuse of a man – excuse because he put up with this – lying there beside tiny brothers, all the time waiting for his old fella to spew his yellow guts over the top of them.

How did he expect I would reply to this? Was I being sent up in some way? Did he try out this routine with all his mates? I realised in a flash how few friends he had. Why? Was it by necessity to keep other men at a serious distance, since he'd realised, probably by instinct, not to trust them? Maybe these revolting memories were what he'd learned to recite to impress the ladies – but how would such sickening tales win them? Their sympathy perhaps, their pity? Well, I could not oblige, I'm afraid. The best I could give him back was a simple bit of advice. I said maybe you should stop drinking. Give it a rest, bit by bit – one drink at a time, as they say.

He did agree that made sense. It would not even be that hard to pull it off, he admitted. He could manage fine without getting himself wasted. Was tonight not proof? Look at him, a happy man, sitting without a drop of the hard stuff in front of him, not minding in the slightest, wasn't that right? He raised his voice, repeating, isn't that right, boy? Are you listening – have you got an answer? Speak up, boy. I'm not your boy, I never will be, don't call me that, I said, getting to my feet.

He apologised instantly. What had come over him? He didn't know what. That happens a lot to you, I challenged him. That's when he asked me what I made of Louise. I told him. I thought she was a decent girl. He might treat her with a bit more respect if he had any chance of keeping her. Keep her, yes, he nodded, that's one way of putting it. I want to keep her. Marry her, he confided, what do you make of that?

I pointed out it was a bit sudden. A bit of a leap from asking her out for a drink or a meal. A bit more than a quick court, you mean? he asked. So, tell me, will she take me, do you think? And he was serious. He appeared as if he really wanted to know. I pointed out I'd barely met the lassie, how could I tell him if she thought herself ready to take the plunge, and would she take it with him? He let me realise in no uncertain terms how much he'd value my opinion since I seem to be the one person who appeared to give a damn whether he lived or died. What about Louise? Does she not give a damn? Yes, Louise, he murmured, are you jealous? I have my own way with women, I laughed, why be jealous of you? Not me, he said quietly, her – I mean are you jealous of her?

That's when he decided it time to have another pint, or maybe a small one. I thought it best to leave him there, for if I'd stayed five minutes more in his company, the law of the jungle decreed that big and brawny as he was, I would need to let his teeth feel the power of my fist because of what he'd just implied. I didn't do that, because I was still in a state of near shock at the ramifications of what he threatened. And why had he accused me? I decided he clearly wanted rid of me so he could get sozzled. Why else ask what he had asked? Did he expect that I would be muggins enough to take it on my good self that I talk him out of staying put in a bar that was now filling and so stop him getting seriously drunk again? Or did he think I minded about a tosser who did not give a tuppenny curse who he was insulting as soon as he started stewing in his cups?

If he did, he thought wrong. I might not be able to

parade a sot of a father as my excuse for losing the rag on the beer. I might not possess a mother busy displaying her bruises as evidence for her part in the war against Irish womanhood. I might treat what girlfriends I could number with a modicum of courtesy. But I did not have as easy and lazy a life as he might he thinking, and I had too much gumption in me to let this shit continue threatening me and simply sit back listening to his insults. I knew that now was the time to bid a rapid farewell. If he believed he'd driven me out, then what in hell odds did I care what he wanted to think? I raced out of there, not looking back.

I heard him saying, wait for me, I'll come with you – listen, don't take it thick, I'll come with you. Well, he could whistle Dixie as far as this boyo was concerned. If he broke his neck staggering home, let him. Not my call. Then he started to call after me in his fluent French – what he said I couldn't decipher, but it was much to the amusement of the pub's other customers. They'd started bellowing '*Je T'Aime*', accompanied by seriously heavy breathing. Matthew just stood, holding his ground, as we were both humiliated, listening to the crowd panting as they invented words to the song, all the time making love with their mouths, their black pints spilling out in their shaking, sour hands.

Thank Christ I escaped the tail end of that debacle. I don't know how long O'Loughlin stuck it out, but if I'd needed more proof this was a man to avoid at all costs, I now had it. I could not sleep, for the events of the night were playing out my nerves more than I dared admit. The silence of that bedsit, without television or radio, there were winter nights it drove me a little crazy, longing for any company, but in the early hours of this morning I was never as glad as now to be on my own, for I was asking questions I needed to answer myself. I could not as yet even put what I meant into words, so how would I solve the riddles life was posing me? That's when there was a knock at my door – two, three in the morning.

I opened it, knowing who was there. He was perfectly capable of raising hell through the block of flats. Dreading he'd enter, but I had no right to disturb people's night sleep. He was swaying, and I have to say this did surprise me a bit, there was a little smile on his face. Can I come in? he asked politely, and continued in a low voice, saying, this is some night I can tell you, shot down twice, first you, and then her. I didn't shoot you down, I corrected him, I left you to go to hell, taking yourself and your insults with you. Well, she did reject me, she wouldn't have me, Louise, not a chance, he informed me, she said no, no, a thousand times no.

Could you blame the woman? I asked him. But it was as if he no longer heard. He just kept repeating the words no, no, a thousand times no. For some reason he found this immensely funny and started giggling to himself. He suddenly stopped laughing, turning his full attention to me, asking could I blame her? I went to where she lives, he told me, I stayed as long as I could, and Louise point blank refused me. I told her I couldn't take no for an answer – then her flatmate hauled her into the sitting room out of the hall where she was keeping me and said she was calling the guards or the neighbours, her brother was a boxer who lived five minutes away and he would fix me right and proper. I don't know if she was telling the truth, but I made myself scarce. I thought it best. Are you going to keep me here at the doorstep all night? Can I come in?

He was already inside, standing six foot strong in the one room that had been my shelter for the past two years I'd worked in this border town. I'd collected next to nothing about me in that time – a few books, a bad drawing I'd done of myself, a single poster advertising a Viking exhibition in the British Museum from my first visit to London. Not much, but my own. If he'd looked for money, I had a few notes tucked into the pages of Blake's poetry I would have given him had he asked, and I'd close the door gratefully after him. But he didn't – he wondered had I anything strong in the flat?

He'd plonked himself now on a chair, sitting, his long legs sprawled. Even a bottle of stout would do me, he confided. I have nothing for you, Matt, I warned him, not in your condition. He asked why I had begun to call him

Matt, was he not always Matthew to me? He admitted he'd always preferred Matthew, and he would let me in on a secret – he really loved being called Matthieu, it was one of the reasons he chose to study French, to have the happiest year of his life hitchhiking through the country, picking up bits and pieces of work, learning this beautiful language in which he became a different man, freer, more gentle maybe, knowing himself and his nature in ways he would never have imagined it possible back where he and his breed had settled and thrived like the bad weed they were. Do you always wear pyjamas in bed? He suddenly wanted to know.

We never had them, too poor, he laughed as if this was the greatest joke of the night. Do you know who gave me my first pair? A farmer's son when I'd stopped over for grape picking on a farm near Bordeaux. He saw me sleeping in my skin. Must have taken pity on the poor Irish boy. I didn't want to seem ungrateful, but they were damned uncomfortable to wear if you're not used to donning a jacket and trousers to sleep in – and he kept asking were they the right size. What do you think he was after?

Nothing probably, I told him, maybe he was just being generous. Nobody's that generous, he retorted, particularly in France. He said that was why he liked them. Always and ever on the make. Best way to be. Obliged to no one. He left the jimjams, as he now called them, on the bed when he left the farm. Maybe the farmer's son, he'd treasure them. Why the hell should he? I demanded. People are funny in that way – odd – look at Louise. She'd laughed in his face when he proposed. Can you credit that? he asked. I told her I meant it. She grabbed me by my balls and tweaked my micky, she said that's all you're getting for tonight, mister – come back again and we'll see what's what in that department, but I wouldn't bank on you receiving more.

She didn't do that, did she? Stop fucking lying, I nearly shouted at him, I've had enough of you. I'm hitting the hay, wander off home. Stay in that chair, wank yourself stupid. Don't ever call here again. For now and forever give my head peace. Let me sleep. I switched off the light. I climbed into bed. And exhausted, I now slept soundly, hearing him snore his head off.

His arm is around my waist. When did that happen, am I dreaming or what? His hands go to my pyjama cord. His tongue slips into my mouth. What does it taste of? Dirty soup. His lips, they start to strip me naked. He holds me where I hold myself. His fist pounds my head down. He fills me with blood. His knife is what he carries between his legs. He opens me wide. He cuts me. I hear him push me from him in a single roar. He leaps. The bed is oozing. He stands there, shrinking. He is breathing from his mouth the word animals. We are animals, he weeps.

I left the school that summer. Afterwards I kept minimal

contact. By chance I got word a few years later he did get married – not to Louise – and he had a son.

I got it into my head last year it would be safe to google his name and where we'd taught to see was he still serving his time in that same school. I learned he'd been promoted – second-in-command, his face, now spectacled, beaming out at me. He is also well respected in his teachers' union, making relevant points about working practices at conferences. I would not dream of ringing and reminding him – would he even remember?

Perhaps if I went insane, I could leave a message, say on his mobile, should I chance upon his number. I might bark like a dog. Howl like a wolf. Roar like a lion. Some noise that might convey to him, that me and my like, we have started to hunt in packs and we are coming, knowing where his trail leads. We can still smell his voice, his sweat, his blood.

But should I shout out, I know where you hide, I will chase you, running behind, bringing you the wages that you deserve, staining you for life, robbing you blind – marking you man for man, beating you to pulp, whispering in your ear, animals, animals.

JANE AUSTEN IN IRELAND, 1845

D ear friend, I thought you might be interested in this oddity I stumbled upon recently. As you know, our classes in local history are a focal point of involvement between this college and the community. Since the launch of our diploma course we have seen the number of students spiral, as return-to-education applicants avail of our excellent opportunities to reacquaint themselves with learning skills.

I keep my eye out for anything remotely eccentric or strange that comes my way. It helps me to retain interest in the various topics students choose as subjects for their theses, as it was far from the field patterns of Longford or the price of heifers and the payment of church tithes in Mullingar that I did my research. For my sins I investigated the transition in monarchy from Elizabeth I to James I in seventeenth-century England and Scotland.

My prime concern was the developing language of religious extremism under both rulers. When I first came to this university – then it really did operate as a university should – that is the very era I was appointed to teach. Now if you were mad enough to express an interest in the life and times of what we nicknamed Liz and Jack, you might be whipped into studying with the country and western expert who shares her teaching duties between music and English. Who would have thought there could be so much in the lyrics of Dolly Parton? Her descent from Ulster Protestants does no harm in these academically ecumenical times. Yes, who knows what codes lie hidden in the ballads, rhymes and refrains of that Tennessee lady?

I digress. I repeat I am now running this local history course. Literacy is not a requirement. An address in the vicinity of the college is adequate qualification. Even a grandparent born within yodelling distance of our hearing would be sufficient. Would you believe we were once considered to be a seminary of sorts? There are now no religious barriers. Indeed you would be welcome garbed in the robes of a Hare Krishna monk, so desperate are we for numbers. I do believe we might fall on you were you to present yourself donned in the full regalia of the Ku Klux Klan. Particularly if you can discern a connection between the Klan and the linen mills of the Irish Midlands. Perhaps the mills provided the Klansmen with low-priced sheets.

PAPRIKA

Among the gems of human knowledge I have so far this year examined include button moulding in Tinahely; the use of turf in Leixlip during the Second World War; and, my personal favourite, the history of a family thimble passed down to the present day.

I am expected to smile interest in heirlooms, extensive epistles from England, multitudes of missives from Scotland, a mountain of letters from America – Jesus, I wish even one of the tribe had gone to the wilds of Wales – photographs of works' outings, the recently discovered minutes of County Monaghan Council meetings 1953-1982, and indeed I do smile, for what I cannot doubt is the sincerity behind all this showing, all this telling. I must resist imagining I put a match to it all, because it is evidence of a sort that the people who were before these people did create them and pass on what history could be passed on – even if that were worth next to nothing.

How could I give such an evaluation to my students? How could I be so brutally honest and say, you are wasting your time? Well, I could when I realised what some of them were up to. The cheek of it, the cruelty of it – I was deeply shaken. I was furious. Of course, I know all about the tittle-tattle of college life. In some departments you cannot fart without someone ringing for the fire brigade. This I can live with. But some things are not up for the analysis of wagging tongues. And my marriage ending is one of those things.

All right, it happened sixteen years ago. He left Ireland for some ridiculous college in the States. I'm sure he
works in the type of science faculty where Darwin has
never been mentioned. I've heard he married a mutual
friend of ours. I believe they had babies. She never had
my figure to boast, so I do trust she kept her shape. He
had no longing for children when he was hitched to me,
and I can confirm none of this because I have no contact
with this ludicrous pair and I want to know nothing about
the bastards. People soon learned not to mention either's
name in my company. If they did, I stood up, walked away
and kept my dignity. One day I realised I could not do this
if I were in a plane. I believe that, to a day, is when I first
grew terrified of flying. This didn't help me get to conferences where so many contacts are made, particularly in
the publishing world. That's why I had no book, and no
book, no promotion. This is the lying bastards' fault. Still,
I do not blame them for my demotion to local studies.
Yes, I suffered but so did the entire department, the entire
university. No, I will not – must not get started on what is
happening to education, for I would not get to the point
of what upset me so much.

I suppose every department has its monster – the sad
lunatic who could only have made a living in the asylum
of academia. I am not that monster. I pride myself on
being accessible to staff and students alike. I do run a tight
ship. Deadlines should be met. Essays should be clear and,

preferably, concise. Tears, which might work for a man, harden my heart. Familiarity is met with a mixture of who the fuck are you and who the fuck am I? I am distant and defiant of any intimacy with female or male. That was why the woman's sympathy shocked me.

She had the grin I associate with women older than myself still surprised to be doing exams at their age. They do not so much come carrying apples for the teacher as dentures to help you chew. I resist my impulse to bite these weird sisters and prove I still have my own teeth by raising my voice a little higher and keeping my tongue deep down in my mouth. For some reason this technique gives me the reputation that I am a genuine sort of person – I have never worked out why. They all mistake vocal contortions for a maternal instinct. I lack in that respect. Perhaps this individual, showing me the documents, suffered from the illusion that I would be touched by her mother's history. As I am telling this story because of her and those papers, I suppose she was right.

As I have said, any oddity, anything out of the way I have come to treasure. I suppose a poem, and in particular a long poem, qualifies as an exotic treasure. Mind you, they are not altogether rare. I was once presented with an eight hundred-line litany of rhyming couplets in praise of Athlone, princely Athlone – to where I'll return wher'er I roam. I did feel duty-bound to inform the author's nephew that even if his dead uncle had received

an education, William Butler Yeats would not be quak-
ing in his boots.

This lady's tale was rather different. I'll call her Mrs
O'D—. For all her ingratiation to me, I'm sure she would
want to protect her anonymity. I don't know why I
believe that. Perhaps it is down to my thorough dislike
of the woman and my suspicion of her motives. She gave
me her wares with the charming observation that she and
her like so enjoyed my attachment to what they'd pool
from their past, I was such an historian, so encouraging
them to rifle through the chests and suitcases, the boxes,
the drawers, and find what had been forgotten. She dared
to venture that my kindness in appreciating – what did
I appreciate – their tribal gongs and identity cards, their
knick-knacks and keepsakes, well, wasn't it obvious why?

I had nobody belonging to me. I was alone. Oh, for the
love of fuck, spell it out. I had no man. What jokes did
they crack among themselves about this barren old bitch
stretching her days out in a redundant, ridiculous, run-
down waste of a department whose college had not so
much seen better days as buried them in an unidentified
place and could not even dance on the grave. That was
because – stop using that word, that excuse, *because* – it
implies a logic – it assumes that what was done was right
in the first place.

It wasn't. This is not the place for pleading special causes.
My kind-hearted student asked if I would cast an eye over

these pages and judge whether there was material for a thesis here. They had been passed down to her through the family's female line. Not a mother nor a grandmother but some class of aunt. That was as much as she could establish. From centuries ago. Well, the mid-1860s. This aunt had been in service to a family called Lefroy, well-to-do, more than well-to-do, and the children were notorious throughout Ireland for not marrying. Even I knew of that legend, the loveless Lefroys. They simply refused to marry, handed the estate over to the nearest of their father's relatives, and I know I heard their mother was responsible for their absolute reluctance, to a woman and man, to consider marriage. All of the daughters clearly suffered from what we would describe as self-mutilation – one even wrote letters to another in her own blood. Here before me now was this fool of a student, she who pitied me, but displaying invaluable evidence from the mother of this brood, an epistle in verse – very loosely structured verse. Identifying herself, speaking to her husband, her children, her sister, even to the Irish people themselves, Protestant and Catholic, and dating the letter with that mystical year 1845, the beginning of the Famine.

When I am asked, as an historian, what do you make of the Irish Famine, I reply, a lot less money than those who made a living whinging about it. The only mystery that surrounds it for me is how long it took this race to start profiting from it. There is so much that is filthy in this nation's destiny but the greed of Irish gombeen men and shopkeepers throughout that horrendous time of hunger, it still takes the breath away. When I watch the game of hurling, I cannot bear to refrain from saying that it is the soul of this country. The game thrived in certain counties through the generosity of landlords. Lads were well fed to keep up the game's standards, and the much maligned English planters paid the food bills. That way the Brits could still indulge and have a good day's gambling as the hurlers cracked shit out of each other. Paddy's survival came down to a spat between, say, Offaly and Wexford. Jesus, on the pitch they'd kill each other. Still, it was good sport. Good man, good man.

I doubt if the sender of this letter had ever set eyes on a good game of hurling. She certainly makes no mention of it. Yet, she had contact with her peasant tenants. This is pretty clear. But I take too long to get to the point – you want to read the letter, the poem, the communication from this woman. She deliberately calls herself Jane Austen, her maiden name, and not Mrs Tom Lefroy. This is surprising. Tom Lefroy rose to the highest rank in the Irish judiciary, but as is obvious, she wishes to disassociate herself from his career. Read into that what you will, but don't read too much.

If I am to be any help, might I suggest that much of what you do read is, well – the lies of an imaginative woman. A fiction. A silly grumble. Everything should be taken with a dose of salt. She is excellent at evading any criticism of herself. She shifts from subject to subject with a rapidity of reference that shows a lively mind, but the merest touch with the Lefroys' chronology indicates that this woman was – must be – in her seventies – even in her eighties. The occasional wildness in her tones, the vulgarity, the nonsensical claims to adultery – perhaps even lesbianism – these all indicate a propensity to the fantastic. This is a roundabout way of saying that the Lefroy woman was incapable of telling anything but lies. Truth was a stranger to her, this Miss Austen.

That, naturally, does reduce the historical validity of the writing. But there is no doubt that it will amuse the experts of the time – the poetry of the time. Yes, I've shown it to the experts. Well, to one. I adored his smile as he read the poem. I enjoyed the concentration. He remarked that while it was clear the science of metrics was beyond this woman's, this Austen's, intelligence, she was capable of striking images, marshalled into prose, masquerading as poetry.

I leave it now for yourself to read. I give it the title she did.

'Jane Austen in Ireland, 1845'

I married Tom Lefroy at first asking.
Six healthy youngsters leapt from our strong loins,

As strange as crocodiles, but one stuttered.
A tie of the tongue disabled my son –
Our idiot boy, my husband mocked him,
Not knowing the lad had no Lefroy blood.
I put my crime down to sweet amnesia
Afflicting the gentry and poor alike.
I will be forgiven by all in the know
What it is to be married in Longford.

The Irish welcomed me in their fashion,
Big con of a bride from the English shires –
Her skinflint dowry fifty pounds exact –
All she had to stand between her and heaven,
Beggar on horseback or donkey and cart,
Tethered to the rock, fed on Longford gorse.
My husband's tenants brought their gift of dance
At crossroads to celebrate our union,
But I worshipped at a different steeple.

I chased with the hounds to pluck from hare's bells
The dreams of old women when they were young –
Fragile bones ready to break in the palm
Young Tom Lefroy hands the parish spinster.
The lassies with land and fair bits of tin,
He showed them the gate, chose this specimen
To wax and wane in her auburn days
Controlling her brood in County Longford,

PAPRIKA

Their fate in accord with steeple-crazed stars.

Thus was my duty well executed.
Do not complain tending garden and house.
Dandelions thrived, the children wet beds
At the green touch of my poisonous fingers.
I sat still at the margins of my life
To create havoc at its centre. Laugh,
And the world fears you. Weep, you weep alone.
A house-trained wife, not pissing on carpets,
I learned the native wit. Knife in your back,
Shite on your flowers – planters, flee Longford.

My Irish accent entranced my husband,
Then bored his arse rigid as frying pans.
I was instructed in the art of bread
Baked from wheat grown in fields rarely crossed.
These fields were not my province, not a women's
Province, a woman bearing to Longford –
Remember, fifty pound – a tidy sum
In no one's language, least of all Lefroy.
When the sixth swan hatched from my shell-like ear,
I heard no song of praise. He was not there.

Desertion pleased me. A childless village.
I'd turn into a prancing girl in pinnies,
Dying for her first ball to take the breath

Away as crocodiles do, drinking dry,
Dangling at my breast, devouring my slice
Of time, my hope, my faith, my charity –
My fair share of good works throughout Longford.
My petticoat muddied, my skirt stained, I read
The good book to scavengers, feeding God
To folk who hungered only for a way out.

In starvation who might they resemble?
A well fed lady growing into fat?
A perfect match for the ox she married?
The stout Anglican who'd bury his wife
Alive for heresy, for infections
Caught from the spit of pagans at prayer –
Infidels dying beneath stark windows
Down dirty laneways of County Longford,
Crying for milk from the lord and master.
Feed us a bite for sweet love of Jesus.

I can't say how he'd react had he lived
To hear my tale. I'd dished up six of the best,
Danced him to his grave, then was left to rot
Far from kith and kin in the wilds of Longford.
I should have taken arms then, upped camp, bag
And baggage, did a runner back to England –
Not a sinner there with welcoming arms
For the warrior home after hardship,

The parson's daughter, last of her tribe.
I call upon my sister's shade to rise.

Prophetess of doom, Cassandra answered.
Women, there's better than cradle and cock.
I'm poisoned in the face repeating that–
You'll rue the day you skite cross the Irish Sea,
Selling your silver to thieves in the night,
You who could carry candles to heaven.
He'll write down your name in red pen and ink –
That's you for the chop in County Longford.
Something is stalking that neck of the woods.
It dines on your belly, your bone, your brains.

Her screech was a bird reading its entrails
Warning the future Jane Austen Lefroy
She'd do the dirty six times in her life,
An English rose transplanted to Longford,
Taking well to days of fire and brimstone.
Her children's servants still remember
The bucket of soil she swore came from Sodom
Where she'd cut her teeth, where she was heading –
Strange in its way as her devilish habit,
Smiling when laughter was quite unseemly.

There the despatch ends. I know next to nothing about
judging poetry, and absolutely nothing about writing –

neither did this woman. From what I can find in our library and a quick scan of the internet this seems to be all that survives of her literary efforts. In my humble opinion her loud silence up to and after this outburst of lament is no great loss. Her metres are higgledy-piddledy. Her syntax lacks – I was going to say signs of sanity. The silliness of some of her imagery – children as crocodiles – the confusion in her time schemes, in her thinking, they betray some signs of Alzheimer's. The contempt for her husband and children is genuine. This was clearly not a happy family. It does not surprise me that her sons and daughters, passionately embraced a life of celibacy. And what about the ending? Creating a sister called Cassandra is a trick of a classically trained mind, but isn't it a rather obvious trick? What interests me more than the content here is the history of its survival.

It seems the forgotten ancestor who lay hands on this material also obtained some books. These were placed reverentially on a shelf, specially mounted on the wall beneath the scarlet lamp illuminating the Sacred Heart of Jesus. Prayers were said nightly to ask for the protection of the icon as the family knelt before it. The Protestant lady who wrote the hidden text, was she turning in her grave as rosary after rosary was recited? Her loathed, unfortunate husband must be smiling in his afterlife to hear of her punishment – her last will and testament trapped in a poor cabin subjected to the superstition of his peasants. What did they make of this mad reversal of fortune? I asked my beaming student. She was now convinced I share her fascination with this worthless scroll.

They were too frightened to read it, she confesses. It was a terrible scandal one of this Catholic clan went to work for the other side. While they were very good and kind to this particular aunt, she would have been better fit never to have darkened the door and gone instead to work for a family who dug with the same foot as herself. The books were never opened until the student herself was a child and for the first time everyone in the house could read and write. The poem was pressed into the pages of a volume of verse by Cowper. My student had brought it and the rest of the books to be valued by a second-hand bookseller. He mentioned a miniscule sum that she considered insulting, so she took them back home. This was when she first looked carefully at the tiny handwriting, barely legible, written on the inside of the envelope containing the poem. She could just about decipher what it said. It read, this is my mother's curse on all her children.

My student showed it as a joke to her mother. She should have known better. Mother was devout. She demanded this curse be taken straightaway to the local priest and blessed with holy water. It would bring bad luck if it weren't dealt with immediately. Mammy dear, this has been sitting on that shelf for decades – it's been passed down from your grandparent.

This cut no ice with her mother. We didn't know what it was then. We do now. I have no quarrel with the books as such, she added, I have never had any quarrel with learning. It's what's written in the curse. That's why I want neither art nor part in it. Now do what I tell you and bring it to the priest.

You haven't read it, her daughter retorted, how can you be frightened of something you've not read? It's only a poem.

–It's accursed and I don't need to read it. I don't want it.

–You know nothing about this woman. Nobody does. I've searched high and low for anything connected with her. I've had no luck.

–You will have no luck, never have luck if you have anything more to do with this dirty old poem. I'm sure the language is filthy. Don't ask me to read it. Get it out of my house.

The daughter refused to obey her mother. She would not shame herself by marching to a priest's house, to his door, and asking him if he would read something scrawled down centuries ago because it was giving her mother the willies. Well then, the mother declared, she would go herself. Let's call the mother Annie, the daughter Josie, and the priest Fr Barney.

Annie presented herself to Fr Barney. He asked how she, his old pal, was faring. She said something unusual was bothering her. He knew she meant business when Annie took out a knife and fork to remove the pages of the poem from her shopping bag. She placed them side by side on the table. He went to touch them after she asked him to read but she begged him not to lay a finger on these pieces of paper so frail they were barely there.

Annie insisted Fr Barney do as she bid him. Read this and tell her what to make of it. I can barely see what it says, so I don't know what worries you about it, he defended himself, for he knew the poor woman was genuinely agitated by its contents. Is it something smutty? she asked, something that could burn down the house? Would God send a bolt of lightning and destroy us all for having such a contraption in her home? By this stage the priest had eked out whatever meaning he could from the poem. It seems to me to be a load of nonsense – a complaining woman with more time and money than sense, Fr Barney reassured Annie. Nothing – absolutely nothing to worry her head about. Why get into such a flap about a ridiculous piece of writing in the first place?

There's a curse on it, she explained. Look at this envelope where it was found. Annie actually handled it, forgetting to use the knife and fork, giving it over to the priest. Look what it says – this is my mother's curse on all her children. It puts the heart sideways in me, Father.

–What have I preached from the pulpit in this town about curses?

–They come back upon the cursers, but this is a mother cursing her own children, and that is something that frightens me. I don't know what to do about it.

The priest advised her to go home and bury it back where it had laid for so many years and forget about it. She couldn't do that. Annie was sorry but no, it was really playing on her nerves and if she admitted why, the priest would think she was entirely mad. He told her she was first and foremost always a sensible woman. Speak out.

Though she was not an educated woman, though she had hopes her children might better themselves through schooling, still and all there was one date in Irish history she and everybody else knew by heart, and that was 1845. A glimpse at the title alone convinced her that was when this was first composed. God forgive her, but if that thing was a curse, called by a mother on her daughters and sons, could this poem have caused the blight – the Great Famine itself of 1845? Was there something so unnatural in this piece of writing that the soils and clay, the rain, the wind, and the sun shining over the country, they'd turned sour and barren, refusing nourishment to its family of Irishmen and Irishwomen?

The priest congratulated the woman on her imagination, but felt he had to speak bluntly. She was entirely losing the run of herself when it came to this matter. He had been going to advise her she tear this poem in pieces and be done forever with it. But now he was going to change his mind – he had to for her own good. She must keep it, put it back into its envelope, back into the shopping bag and carry it home. There she was to return it exactly where it all began. Who else knew about this? Josie, her daughter. Josie was to see her do all of this. She was to be witness to how Annie had chased all this dangerous daydreaming out of her head. Annie had to promise she would do exactly that.

Her mother did exactly that, Josie explained to me, but it was the closest the woman ever came to committing a sin of disobedience against a priest. This she confessed to her daughter, who was in her way now confessing to me the whole saga of her family's connection with this author of the poem and her centuries-old outburst.

I listened to her patiently, patiently enough to recount in as much detail as I have, recalling the drone of her midlands accent, flattening everything into its curious one note, slipping so occasionally into two when at its most passionate. She then did something quite extraordinary. She offered me the manuscript. The poem itself. She'd like it to be in careful hands. There were no strings attached. She just wanted – wanted it to have a good home, she laughed.

I did not rise to the bait. I thanked her for her generosity, but it was impossible to accept. I told her I believed all historical materials, even the most esoteric – I did not say useless – should be deposited in archives or in the family vault where they belonged. She pointed out this did not belong to her family, so I strongly advised she leave it not in the college library but in the local one, as this effusion really was only concerned with a domestic matter. Are the family still around? I asked.

They had no descendants, remember? There might be very distant cousins, she wasn't sure. She was sure, though, that she could not trust this to the parish library. A gang of young ruffians used it. It wouldn't last five minutes, even if it survived all these centuries against the odds with nobody belonging to it, to protect it. She would hold onto the manuscript for the time being. She apologised nicely for showing it to me. I told her – I reassured her – there was no need. It was worth throwing an eye over it, but I doubt if there was sufficient matter here to cover the detail and density of a 5,000-word thesis.

She thanked me. 'Jane Austen in Ireland, 1845' would go back into its box. Its book, I corrected her, didn't you find it in a book? Yes, of course, she had found it there. I was right. And she was sorry. Why was she sorry? Sorry I might have found all this ridiculous – a woman called Jane Austen caused the Irish Famine, in 1845.

PAPRIKA

If you were to put a gun to my head and demand I tell you what I believe to be the loveliest aria in all opera, I think I would surprise you. You could not guess my answer in a million years. I can hear obvious choices being recited. Perhaps you would be able to show off and tell me it is some hidden piece buried in an obscure work that you chanced to hear in some little village festival held in the wilds of Ireland, or you stumbled upon this treasure buried in the white throat of a soprano, hired to cultivate a love of opera in the reclaimed wetlands of some obscure Dutch province, where they have, against all the odds, constructed what passes as a concert hall. Maybe I too, by pure luck, discovered this wonderful gem, and here I am, sent to agree with you, to confirm your choice, to prove that there is fate, a force of destiny intent on bringing us together, we who share such an esoteric taste when it comes to beauty.

You would be wrong to assume so. I take no pleasure

in closing that gate to you. I do not allow you to enter, invited, through to my room – make yourself comfortable, kick your shoes off, you know what we like to listen to there. But you cannot be my welcome guest for you don't have permission to come into my house, my company. I do not give you the key. I do not know who you might find prowling there, walking the feet off himself, tiring the day and night out of his limbs so that sleep might at least – a little sleep might even be possible. Who knows what exhausted breathing might follow your footsteps? Who might be on the very brink of expiring in your arms should you dare to cross my threshold? Better to be refused entry – to be denied any access. So as I say, I do not give it to you and already I owe you an apology for misleading you.

This is how I madden my friends. I make a statement that I am about to reveal something about myself – then I stand back at the last minute and say nothing. It is an appalling habit. Perhaps it accounts for my coldness. For why I rarely married. Women's flesh now bores me, and men's has always disgusted me. I live apart. I am honest enough to admit that I prefer the sound of my own voice. Am I alone in making clear that preference? When it comes to my voice, am I flattering myself when I say it is in demand? I shall not bore you with the names of leading companies where I have performed and continue to perform. There is a type of singer whose list of roles is their sole topic of conversation. You can hear their contralto sweetness even as I accuse. A little of that company is sufficient. Whatever else may be made of my arrogance, I can argue I learned my lesson well from these ladies. I avoid talk about my art when I can.

I admit this is because I find so few people capable of interesting me on the subject – they simply lack the verbal accuracy to speak with any degree of intelligence about music. It descends always into what I truly despise – gossip, which is all most criticism comes down to, if truth be told. The squalid daydreams of some silly queen longing to try on a diva's frock, masquerading as the lush lyricism of a Puccini expert, dying to expire as Butterfly, pining onto death for his Pinkerton. Then there are the academics. The odour of pipes, the grey of their beards, the rot of their teeth and breath, the unreadable analysis, the technical mysticism, all of it hiding the deepest ignorance, disguising the simple truth – they do not understand their subject. Inevitably, by their side, the not quite pretty girl or boy, accompanying the ageing master, ever ready for the ride, the kamikaze screw that will disfigure them for life, disfigure them sufficiently to take up the teaching profession.

That is why I make a point of never thanking my teachers. I have been known to race from funeral services rather than to shake the hand of any one of them. I once risked nearly jumping into the open grave to avoid these creatures. I would certainly never go to any of their farewells. I did hear of a Jamaican professor whose relatives insisted his mourners, family and friends, his former pupils, actually dig the earth he was to lie in – I do not fancy dirtying my soft hands in that way. Certainly not for anyone who wasted my time and energy. They all know this. I have never received even a word of congratulations from that jealous shower. It is not that I need nor have looked for such encouragement. I presume my observation, made in an interview, deeply offended. I dared to say I succeeded despite them. Yes, I know it is the kind of predictable joke a clever schoolboy might crack. I was never acknowledged to be clever as a boy. I was never considered special in any way. My instrument was judged to be merely promising, and not especially so. There were fellows in my class who were expected to surpass me. They are now instructing beginners. So, if it were a juvenile insult, I am the happier for that. Really, do they need to take it so seriously? I heard – believe me, I so frequently heard – that I had hurt them. Well, it was my intention to do so. They might have believed that as I aged I would mellow and recover the modesty they had so abused in my childhood and teenage years, suffering under their complacency, learning what took me too many years to discard as utterly worthless in pursuit of my full voice, my full soul and self. They could whistle for all I cared. Not my way, I'm afraid. Not my style.

And what is that? I like perfection. And to me, the perfect piece of music, the one I would most like to sing – it is in the very opera I came to deliver in the Big Apple. This is not my first Otello. I shall not reveal to you how many times I have sung it. It is obvious there are only so many performances one voice can dispatch in that role. Suffice to say, I am not within spitting distance of that total. It is imperative to let your Iago and Desdemona know this. You do so by allowing them to believe that for all your fame, your reputation, your stature, your size – you are a jolly fellow, you are a good sport. I tell them, truthfully, my favourite aria is 'The Willow Song', Desdemona's pathetic cry before she is strangled, as she remembers a maid called Barbara, a girl martyred by a lover who has now deserted her and left her to go mad. I am naturally not alone in adoring Verdi's genius as it caresses and disturbs me through that shattering lament. But there must be, I am sure, few celebrated tenors who for the amusement of their fellow troupers can sing it. It is quite extraordinary that now in my hefty fifties, I can resort to a near parody of my boyhood's beautiful voice – even the threatening break – the disfiguring – I can make an uncanny fist of it.

'Piangea, cantando
Nell'erma landa,
Piangea la mestra

O Salce! Salce! Salce! . . .'

Bravo, Iago praises. Brava, the conductor smiles to correct him. Desdemona throws back her golden hair and sings, 'O Willow, Willow, Willow.' Does the silly bitch think I cannot translate '*salce*'? Then I speak, asking as Desdemona does, who is knocking at the door? In ridiculous falsetto, Iago answers as Emilia does, '*È il vento*' – it is the wind. I resume my boyish brilliance.

'Io per amarlo e per morir.
Cantiamo! Cantiamo!
Salce, Salce, Salce.'

I eye Desdemona. I wait for her to translate. I love him and I will die – Let us sing, let us sing – Willow, willow, willow. I wait in vain. She is strangely quiet. She joins in the generous applause but she alone knows I am not joking. She will perform this exquisite hymn to female weakness. The house will listen to a woman abandoned, perfectly pathetic. Then I will arrive onstage, her ravager, her rope around the neck, the beautiful twist and chain of neck, the weeping face, the eyes darkening beneath the pillow. She will not fear that I might actually kill her. No, she will see in my own eyes, hear in my voice that I mock her. I have more regard for my mockery of the role than her sweet relish of its music. I would make a better

Desdemona than she could ever sing, bound and big as I am, perfectly cast as Otello. Desdemona is born to die, and I know how to do it, how to sing her to death. That is my job. That is why when I finished my mimicking party piece, all through rehearsal, she never takes her eyes off me. So attentive is she to me, I am sure word must be spreading through the scandal-addicted orchestra and chorus, there is surely about our attentions all the signs that an affair was beginning.

There wasn't. Our soprano was considered to be a beautiful woman, but I had tired of beauty. I had even begun to dislike it. This occurred when I was friends with a photographer – in those days I was not choosy. The man was effectively a eunuch. I was most fascinated in his many affairs when they were ending. He would tell me in wonderful confidence when each love was on the point of collapse. He would start to profess to her that he had always confused love with sorrow. The women would begin to receive a rose that had started to wither. It would be delivered at exactly the right instant of his discontent with her. Then he would vanish from her life. Vanish completely. As he did from mine – I have little time for confidants.

I did share the secrets of my lovelife with a sympathetic couple in their restaurant – Hungarian – where I would eat alone, scorning any company but that man and his wife. She was first to notice I'd put on a little weight. But

my voice was improving as my girth was gaining. She
advised me not to grow too heavy. She passed on an old
Danube secret. Sprinkle paprika, as much paprika as you
can tolerate, on everything you eat. That controls your
diet. You will eat less. It had the opposite effect on me. I
had found my addiction, my potion, my elixir. I could not
get enough of it. Smear a chicken with paprika. Inside
and outside. The flesh cooks like the sun. I'd devour it.
The spice seemed to break into my bones, my blood, my
brain, into my singing, so that it burned with warmth, it
loved the sound of itself, my music healed the sick and
the lame, it fed the multitude of five thousand after five
thousand, and had plenty left to feed five thousand more.
I had never tasted such a dish. Had never enjoyed such
success. Place a plate of an entire bird, a feast – breasts,
legs, wings, innards – I will eat it in one sitting, and for
my supper I will find notes of such fulfilment, cadences of
such thanks, a voice you will drink like the reddest, most
vivid wine, quench your thirst with the sweetest, most
fragrant white. And I can do this with the lovely, natural
means of paprika – doses of paprika – my spice, my drug,
my magic. I could not do without it. The food, the weight
suited me. Yes, I grew, and so did my art. Notes more and
more marvellous. Offers more and more frequent. Roles
increasing in demand. Paprika – it did me no harm whatsoever. I sang my soul – I do believe a singer must bare his
soul. And maybe that is what they did, the boy and girl, on

Fifth Avenue, making sweet moan.

That is where I saw them, he lying against a yellow wall
of an apartment building. She had her head on his stained
lap. I was walking from the Waldorf – I know it has gone
down, but I still love the old place, gliding through that
golden foyer, the bar's strong, stinging martinis, the bad
manners of the rude staff – none of that has changed
and strangely enough, in New York, that city of constant
crises, I like stability. That's why I enjoy walking everywhere. And I adore its opera house. On my first engage-
ment, the doorman confused me, asking if I were here
with the construction company doing extensive renova-
tions on the building. That was a joke grown soon stale,
sorry I was to have cracked it only once, but never let
forget it. Now in the bowels of the Met, grown so familiar
I might as well have built its nooks and crannies, I love to
trawl through the labyrinths of corridors, so terribly easy
to get lost in, its highways and byways, able to stroll for
miles through the phantom city buried beneath the Lin-
coln Center, giving what might be my best performances
as I serenade the dust and the dead I sense are hiding in
that eerie building. As I ramble there, I imagine I sing to
my dying father, that enormous man grown thin, eaten by
Alzheimer's, endlessly trekking through the corridors of
his hospital, remembering what he alone could remember, starving to death, demanding he'd dine on nothing

but long forgotten food and drink, wishing to give up, for life was now nothing. I hope he can listen to me pour my soul out, knowing he is dead and hears nothing. He is only cinders and ash.

When I myself die I would like my remains to be thrown into the Met's great fountain. I would approve its towering waters to be the only tears shed for me. I have found mourning is a desperate waste of time. My parents would both have agreed with me on that. We're born, we breathe, we die, we're dirt. It is utter nonsense to feel the need to grieve. We should all be cut from tougher rock. Wailing is ridiculous. It is what theatre – what opera – was invented for, so we can dispense with such conduct. The stage is the best place for such behaviour. Weeping is written out for you. You perform, and the task of tears is done. Sorrow is finite here. It is efficient. It is clean. You make your song and dance, and that's it, over. That is why it would be so convenient if I were to pass away on stage in New York at the Metropolitan Opera. Of course that shall not happen. Life is never that lucky. And I have had my great share – my more than fair quota – of luck – my paprika – it has granted me, that sacred powder – all I can wish. Do not ask for more.

What were they asking for, the boy and girl in the street? What was the crying boy wanting? What was his girl listening to, as she sleeps by him, her dreams the stuff of the boy's delirium? Could he be on something? I know nothing about drugs. I detest any lack of control. If I am to admit any addictive weakness, let it be solely paprika. Natural, nourishing, gentle as milk. I would feed it to these hungry children, but they would spit its goodness back at me and even might turn this goodness into something wickedly infected with the saliva of the damned. Is that what they are? Is it some demon who moves through them? I could not tell for sure. The boy's voice was one long litany, a list of gibberish, unrelenting, pouring from his shaking head, her a bag of silent bones, still, always still, asleep on his knees. To my shock I started to believe that his voice was singing in Russian – could it be Russian? No, I could now decipher it was English. He was definitely speaking in English. For some reason I reckoned I should be afraid of his nonsense.

Die boy die stupid fuck
You father what will you do
No child screaming
Ridiculous
Family listen
Hard luck story
Telling fortunes
Do this favour
Bred into you
Be hard honest we are honest
He touched my throat

My cock
My father forgive
Bearing grudge
The bastard denied me
Me chapter and verse
Help me
Help me
Help me
Help me please
Do you know what the smell is
Smelly bastard
Shitty pissy smelly bastard
Sniffing powder
Orange powder
Being asked sure I am
It turns me
Your child turns
Why not ring
Friends
They answer things
Sniffing
Fuck off
Who is she on my lap
Red hair all short
She is who I am
Passing sentence
We recognise you

Singing lessons
Beloved son David
Help me
Help me
Die boy die stupid fuck
You father what will you do
No child screaming
Ridiculous
Family listen
Hard luck story
Telling fortunes

I am walking to the New York branch of Fauchon, my first port of call in Paris, that shop where food is the rainbow, the pot of gold, myrrh and frankincense, all bright with tastes. Hell, I'd pay fifty bucks for a pint of its milk. So much do I adore its delicacies, I'd smear myself with its mustards, perfume myself with its oils. I tread through its pleasure dens slowly, daily, all those classy French people, sitting in Manhattan, sipping coffee. Could I place something queasy in the bottom of those fancy little cups and make them drink paprika? Then they would stand up and fill the air with good cheer, blasting into the neighbourhood the news that I am like them, well fed, content, searching for – searching – looking for – what? I know what I look after. I am a sensible man, who must look after his throat. His precious jewel. His bread and honey. I must stock up on honey – superb for the voice. The jams, the matchless sweet nougats. Now that I more or less disdain drink, they are my reward after the opera. The reason I adore nougat is that I associate it with my childhood. It was cheap as tuppence then. I loved its white chew with the pink stripe. As a child, I could put it between my teeth and pull – such pleasure. My teeth were clean and my tongue was pink. I had to use my tongue and teeth to sing. The boy and girl I noticed on Fifth Avenue, were they turning into something pink and clean? Turning into me? Into my father? My father, he used to enter me in talent shows. The boy and girl, to the best of my knowledge, they do not beg. If I did well in those embarrassments, my father would stay sober – that was how he rewarded me. I've convinced myself this young couple is harmless. My father knew how to make his son feel wanted. The cops do not move them on, despite their frequent noise. But if I failed – if the victor were to be decided by the audience – if the volume of their applause did not merit me the winner – another swayed their fickle hearts, I lost the vote – then I would feel the tightening of my throat as I heard them limit their appreciation, mine by far the best voice on that stage. My father would side with them, angry at my desperation. I want to cross the wide avenue to avoid that pair. My father put it down to my lack of preparation, that's why I lost and he'd see to it I would not eat tonight. I do vow, tomorrow, when I take my daily exercise, I will pass by them until I reach the confectioner. Then I will feast on French sweets.

But nothing drowns his disapproval. He will – I still hear him –hear his voice. He tells me I am a fat, ugly boy. I take after my mother in my grossness. She too had a fragile voice, so-so, forgettable. When he looks at me, when I fail, I am her son. He informs me, I would disown you if you could not sing. And you will disappoint me. We all know your voice will break. It will melt. Like your fat, ugly mother, it will be no more. It will die. I start to laugh at him. I hear my mother in my laughter. We will continue laughing at this fool of a father. Sing.

> Die boy die stupid fuck
> Your father what will you do
> No child screaming
> Ridiculous
> Family listen
> Hard luck story
> Telling fortunes

I stop. Why am I singing this in the middle of Fifth Avenue? Why are people looking? Where are the boy and girl who protect me in this savage town? I have come out without protection. Without paprika. I am at the mercy of my Magyar advisors. What should I do? They say, sing. Go to the opera – sing Otello. That's what you're paid to

do. Do it. They talk sense. I do obey. I find some paprika.
I eat.

Was I not in such good voice tonight? I question myself
because the inevitable compliments from my Desdemona
and my Iago are particularly sincere this evening. I know
of one ancient lady, now long dead, who had a sure way of
unsettling anyone, and letting them know how she would
do it. If you were good, the prima donna would find some
way of upstaging you – a slight cough, a ruffle of a dress,
even if things were going seriously well, a sneeze. If you
were bad, she would be immobile and listen. This night
the pair of them were still as still can be. Perhaps I flatter
myself. It was not at me both were looking, nor were they
listening to my good self, for in true theatrical fashion,
they have surprised everyone. She is an item, with him,
and I rejoice for both, particularly her, as I have now had
time to study her mournful beauty. Shakespeare described
his Desdemona as a white ewe, and myself as a ram tup-
ping her. With her lengthy face that could be measured in
feet if not furlongs, she does have the features of a hungry
sheep. Tonight in 'The Willow Song', her voice soared
into the tiered echelon of the opera house – the yellow
from its gold reflecting like a thousand wedding rings, all
threatening to distort me from what I am. Her rendering
is greeted with some applause, sympathetic in its fashion,
although I am sure many are willing the strangulation

swiftly on its way – a tough shower of bastards at the Met.

It is a mild night in New York. How rarely that occurs. It is a sure sign something is to happen, something that I cannot control. I give myself to the mercy of events. I cannot stop what comes my way in this perfect weather. Relieved, I will walk the shiny streets of Broadway. Who was ever fool enough to believe they were paved with gold? Well, me for one. And I still do. Beneath the rotten, broken pavements, there are rivers of precious metal, a liquid mine of every mineral, some never yet seen before, and that river of Hades rather than the Hudson is what has truly made New York what it is today, the city where we can be what we want to be. I suppose I should be grateful for the dreams it allows me to possess. Millions of others would be, but I have no thanks, for now all the city does is remind me that dreams are my duty, wishes are my work and my art is hard slog until my voice breaks again into the crackle of old age and I am forgotten. Then everything starts to fade all about me. I stop recognising where I am. The streets' neon signs turn to blue water and wash them away. The revels, the carnivals of Times Square do not sound in my deafened ears. I may as well be in the Australian desert as here, so parched and cold is the night now. I see the great glitter and glamour turn to rack and ruin. The buildings, once so handsome, so virile, have been flattened into dead men. But I know how to walk about this apocalypse. I know where to find food, drink and shelter. It is now very, very late but in this wilderness many shops open for twenty-four hours. I will soon come across one. I must have been walking miles, but in this town it is always squares and circles, so I have not strayed too far from my hotel. Indeed, at a distance, who can I see?

It is them – there they are – my little twosome. Both on their feet now. Him this time the quiet one, her gorging her thirst from a bottle of whatever is her choice of poison, as they say in London. And she is loud, screaming some snatch of a pop tune, none of whose words I am able to decipher, for her voice is hideous. Her face a mess of freckles. Her red hair dirty as he is dirty, they sway, and he laughs as she screams, look, look who it is – look, I told you I saw him, you didn't believe me, you didn't believe he would come to us, but I saw him, look. She points me out to the boy. The fat man, the fat man with the beard, she calls out, Santa Claus. It's him.

She runs to me. The boy is now roaring with laughter. Santa – Santa, she repeats. She puts her arms around me. I hurl them aside as if her limbs lanced me. I open my throat. I give her my voice a full, terrifying blast. Fuck you, don't touch me. Fuck you, never touch me. Do not dare touch me.

She is silent for a second. She looks at me as I've ransacked the breath from her body. I've taken her favourite doll and smashed its plastic head in. Then her wail breaks.

Filth bursts from her lips. You fat dick. You ugly queer. You piece of pervert shit. I know you – I know what you are. Cocksucker – cocksucker. I know what you do. Fat fucking dickhead. I know where you live. I can tell the cops. I'm going to tell the cops.

She now resumes crying. He joins in, and in duet they label me, cocksucker, queer, dick, and many times, cocksucking motherfucker. But then in a voice, clear, strong as my own, the boy warns me again, I'll get the cops, you'll see. You'll be sorry, I'll get the cops.

If my career has taught me anything, it is to avoid noise everywhere but on stage. It is unseemly as – as hunger. It is my mission to quell its pangs and I know how to do so. I try to carry about my person a small, plastic portion of my charm, my protector. Paprika. It is what I pour on that red skull, that freckled face, staining it even more orange, telling her, be calm, my child. I christen you Paprika – henceforth your luck shall change, you and your charming lover – the demon who possesses you. I would free you entirely of his powers but that cannot be, for mankind is bound to suffer. We are born to endure. Let me bless you with the shadow of my dust. Protect your sacred self with most holy spice. Here for you is gold, frankincense, myrrh, call them paprika, devour it. Anoint all your senses. Cease your lamentation.

She yells the fat fucker's blinded me. What has he put into my eyes? It's burning the sockets out. What has he done to my eyes?

I look into her face. She is now pleading to her boy-friend, has he blinded me? If he has, don't let me live. Why did you let him do that to my eyes? If I can't see, end my lousy life. Fucking end it. Just put me down – put me down.

I am now well ahead of them. I sneak a look back. She is bawling in his arms, the whimpers mingling with the chant of fat fucker. He reassures her about getting the cops. Their faith in the New York Police Department is not infectious. I feel more than safe enough. I leave them to their revenge. No one could connect me with that pair. I am a respectable gentleman in an expensive overcoat, his silk blue scarf wrapped wisely around the exquisite instrument of his throat, walking to my suite in the Waldorf Hotel, having done a good night's work playing more than a little proficiently one of the most demanding roles in opera. I look for no more credit nor recognition than that. If I had reacted – if I had engaged in any way with those dangerous children I glimpsed who knows what trouble would have followed? And yet I still hear her cry, put me down – put me down. I do believe she moves me. I am sore tempted to sing back.

'Io per amarlo e per morir.
Cantiamo! Cantiamo!
Salce! Salce! Salce!'

I am not vengeful. I keep my silence and stillness. I will not mock nor push myself centre stage. I will let her lament her heart out. I will console her. I will do as certain tribes in Africa do for women wronged beyond remedy. They are led in scarlet procession to a tree that keens. Then she may die nobly by her own hand using her red tresses as a rope to break her unfortunate neck. Neither man nor beast shall lay a claw on her corpse. Left to the exposure of the benevolent sun, its light shall turn her flesh to gold. But this gold does not last. And it turns, not to rust, but to paprika. In smearing her thus, in telling this, I forgive her. Perhaps I save her. So I leave singing. Salce, willow, salce. Willow, salce, willow.

GIVING YOUR CHILD A GUN
FOR CHRISTMAS

When I was a child in the sixties, they did it as a matter of course, parents, give boys a gun for Christmas. Plastic ones, that is. Some could shoot caps, loud and smelly as the devil's farts. But mine was a rifle, white and azure, you could see it shining at night, when the same devil tempted you to bad thoughts about all the colours you could dream. Although he would describe himself as a peaceful man – couldn't fight butter, his brothers dismissed him – my father bought this present for me. Even then, it was at my mother's urging.

One night I heard her voice turn soft as she persuaded, He has to learn to rough it. You have to make a young fellow out of him. Did you have it delicate ever? Did I? That's what you'll buy him this Christmas, and make sure he knows it was you did the giving. So the gift of the gun was to toughen me up, this toy was the answer to all their worries, but it didn't work for I think his heart was not really in it. She would occasionally point to it and ask neighbours could they believe the price they'd paid for the toy? And was it ever used? Barely, they loyally agreed, casting an evil eye in my direction, proof positive as this was I would come to a bad end just as they'd long predicted. It's his father I blame, he should insist, she'd lament, and they'd nod, chanting in unison, I blame his father. Thank Christ she found that vaguely derogatory, them re-echoing her censure, and so the subject was dropped.

Still, everything has its use, and next year at our summer concert our class staged the visit of President Kennedy to Ireland and the warm welcome we gave him. The best looking boy with wavy hair played JFK. One of the teachers patted powder on his face, expecting him to squeal, but he just smiled and looked more beautiful than ever. The biggest lad was his security guard, and to my delight he was armed with my blue and white rifle, a red ribbon tied round its butt as a tribute to complete the flag of the USA. We were packed around the gorgeous leader, welcoming him with rounds of 'McNamara's Band' sung in Irish, waving a cacophony of babies' rattles, as we heard him thank us for this wonderful display in a broad Donegal accent, the Boston twang being beyond our man's dramatic range. He was a looker, but no actor, and so awful in the part, I can still hear him thud his way through his words of welcome – *Céad Míle Fáilte* I hear you say to me, for everyone must speak the Gaelic here at *Féis Ailigh*. I think his security guard disappeared with my rifle – I never saw it again, and neither parent mentioned it, but my father did at times refer to the show as the greatest melder of shite he'd ever witnessed, and it was his belief Kennedy organised his own assassination so he'd never have to come back and witness the like himself. Just as well this was uttered beyond my mother's hearing, because she worshipped John Fitzgerald Kennedy for being a devout Catholic. Wasn't it well known he'd made a point of shaking every nun's hand when he called to the old homestead in New Ross? And she had better things to worry about than missing a child's gun, expensive though it may have been. Weren't they everywhere anyway? Christ knows what use they'd be put to in this country.

All of this is my way of saying I should not have batted an eyelid when I saw a gang crossing over the bridge, one of the boys proud as punch carrying a shotgun like an infant – a metallic infant – slung over his shoulder.

I have always loved the word 'posse', but would that describe this shower since there was no one they could be following, could they? A bit older than me, they had faces I could only put a stutter of names to, ours being a school you didn't dare look straight in the face any fellow in the year above for fear your eyes might offend and you could lose one. Mercy was not a virtue there, though the building was dedicated to the Sacred Heart of Jesus, overflowing with burning love for men according to his hymn, but you might be wise to confine that infatuation to the song. They had, the four of them, the walk of sturdy chaps in splendid possession of what they could not believe would ever land in their sweaty grasp, and so it did not matter where they were headed towards. All that counted was that they could do damage if they so chose, and that damage would be of their solitary making. I must have met each on their own a thousand times – might even have dared nodded if we were in the company of neighbours from the year dot. I knew the history and geography, the whos and whys, the ins and outs, of every gang that could kick the lining out of any who offended them – the offence could be so slight, it might never have occurred – but these hard chaws, they travelled in a troop and reserved a right to deliver a hiding on all who crossed them. They made soup out of mammy's boys. If you were a specky four eyes, they ate your glasses. They took it as a personal slight if they did not make you piss yourself.

Each mob had its own way of humiliating, and none would be so crass as to copy another. Hence you did not think twice of getting on their wrong side. You always and ever quickly learned who had united with whom in pursuit of enemies, real and imagined. Sometimes it broke your heart when friends were found among them.

This meant ties of place, of shared lanes, playgrounds and pitches, counted for nothing anymore. They were lost and gone, no longer to be trusted, and neither could you. You were now the other side. I was always the other side. And while I recognised no former ally or foe in that approaching horde of four, I expected the worse, for that is life.

From where were they coming? I could not say for sure since I cannot give their names as none could be identified, but it must have been from a house and in that house they must have kept a gun they allowed their boys to play with, be it Christmas or not. Thus trusted, they moved at a steady march over the railway bridge where no trains ran under this thirty years or more, and then they took the laneway, where we lived forever. Mammy grew up and spent all her days in that spot, so she knew every inch, every doorstep and every windowsill, every story and every secret whispered, every twist and every turn of the past and its pains and pleasures. She passed all that on to me. There has never ever been a location since then which I can recall with such exactitude – the buildings all the same to the ignorant eye, but the colour on each latch, the state of every curtain, the smell from a hallway, all different, all affected by what happened to each neighbour. They speak for themselves if you can hear accurately. Take your time and look, walk it morning, afternoon and twilight – even dead of night, if your mind is so unsettled you have to get out from the four walls entrapping you that tightly they'd started to climb into your ears, burrowing through wax the stink of which would knock you down if you let yourself smell it, bricks and mortar talking to you, urging you to do what you shouldn't and say what you couldn't, if you wanted to stay put where you belonged, and do the chores assigned to you.

My job there was to fetch milk in an open bottle from my grandparents' house down to our own across the bridge. The Dunbar girls, Hannah and Mary, with their brother Richard for safety on the dark roads where badness lurked, they delivered it from their farm in Conglash, leaving their bicycles parked for safety in my grandparents' porch, if they were going to see the flicks in St Mary's Hall. The milk from their farm, it was the whitest thing in the world. They'd attach tin cans to their handle bars and cycle with such concentration they'd not spill a drop and make no noise arriving – you only knew they were there when they knocked at the door. A quiet family, the Dunbars, my grandmother would compliment them, three civil beings, the girls and the son, harming nobody, minding their own business as we should all do. The boys with the gun, they might not have agreed.

Even as a child, I could see ghosts wherever I looked. Especially as a child, I saw ghosts. Or they saw me, saying nothing menacing, nothing much at all really if truth be told, just gawking in front of me and behind, so don't you forget it. If I spilt the beans how haunted the lane

became the longer I walked down its length, I would not
have been believed. We were rarely believed as youngsters
anyway. But I did bear witness to multitudes as I made
that mighty trek from top to bottom, crossing realms of
the living and dead, never confusing one for the other,
feeling the milk inside the bottle protect me, its wash of
whiteness, the glass like another arm I had no power over,
capable of raising itself and smashing Christ knows where
in a blaze of resurrection should the mood possess it. In
that strange zone where anything may occur, I needed to
map with rigour the stages of my journey home. Then I
could begin to breathe with relief, maintaining this time
I could complete my journey safely, unmolested by angels
or demons fighting their eternal battle for control of the
celestial heavens above my red head and the solid earth
under my brown sandals. Not that it was all that solid.
You knew if it took the inclination, the ground of Donegal could open – you would see all the pitch black of
limbo and the bony bodies of babies, unbaptised, dead,
mouldering, infants sobbing for their mothers beneath
your stockinged feet.

The moon, of course, was no friend to you in this panic.
It brought as much darkness as it shed light from itself like
hairs from a cat. Didn't Nancy Fletcher's father one night
see a cloud following him home? When he looked up he
saw it draw a moustache like Adolf Hitler's on the face of
the man in the moon. He ran home tracked all the way by

the apparition in the sky above him, terrified because he was in Derry when the Germans bombed it and he swore that night, again, he could smell the same fire. Breathless, he stopped to cut the sign of the cross on himself. Didn't the cloud just disappear, or was it the moon? The very stars and planets, they could not be trusted. They too would leave the heavens and harm you. So what were the chances the gun in their hands and itching fingers would be fired and leave a hole big as your arse in your belly?

Highly likely, you'd say, and you could be right, for now we were all reaching the safest spot at night, a lamp post and electric light shining. Reaching there was halfway home. At the middle of my journey, spirits of the air hid themselves from sight under this glare, frightened to be named and shamed, identified in the strange glow. No such fear struck the boys now pointing the gun. They laughed as they caressed it, shouting to each other, where should they fire it? Then they whispered, your man, he can see us, and your man was myself. They could blast my body's eyes from their sockets! I felt my bowels turn to dirt gathering inside me, under my control, yes, but like a loaf of concrete I had somehow swallowed, hard, hard and harder. They raised the gun. They pointed. One shouted, the bottle! Aim at the bottle. Spill his milk on him. But they aim higher. The trigger's pulled. The bullet flies. The lamp fragments. Electric light exploded. What bad omen was this bursting comet? They had found their target – it is not me, not myself, it is not myself.

When I get home, who is there with a face like a fiddle on them asking what it was that kept me? I could have been to Belfast and back in the time it took me to do a simple message. Well, speak up, why am I not answering back? I'm never at a loss for something smart alec. Why am I soaking when it's dry as a bone outside this night? The milk, what happened to it, there's less than half a bottle full? My trousers, they're drenched with it. Well, there's no clean spare pair, I'll have to wear the same tomorrow. What did I get up to? I could be sent to do nothing – trusted to do nothing. Don't dare start crying – we'll be drinking our tea black at breakfast. Did I throw the milk over myself or what? If all I'm going to do is stand there dripping, get up to bed, forget about supper.

Under the covers I listen to whispers from the kitchen. They are millions of miles away. Far off I can hear the music of a showband playing in the Plaza Ballroom on Ferris Lane. That's where they're dancing, the women and the men. I can smell their hair oil and see the lovely shades of their ties. Maybe one is wearing a purple shirt like the teacher in school that day I could not budge myself with shock at what took place inside and outside of me because of the colour.

The bed moves funnily, and I can taste the air which is different than before, singeing, like a lit match. No matter what, I know I've nearly died, but I'm still living, and to prove it I say words I love that I heard on television but don't know what they mean. I just love the sound. 'Cruciform' – 'schism' – 'hex'– 'linear'. I try to turn them into a football chant, the names of all my players, but they do a runner – they are not on my side, I have lost their comfort. They have the faceless faces of the boys shooting a gun. Shooting me if that is how their temper sways in that direction. If I ever dream again, it will be of them, unless I tell what they did, and you can never tell. All hands know that for certain if nothing else.

I sit up in the bed. That hard brick in my belly, it starts to come up my throat. Maybe it's my heart, maybe it is my blood, maybe it is my bones thawing, all looking to escape. To get away from me. Away from what I saw being done. I start to feel my teeth and my lips melt. I try to keep my mouth sealed. Hold it back. It opens in a roar that stings, and the vomit is everywhere, not just on the bedclothes, sheets and pillow cases, the good eiderdown, but all over me, every nook and cranny of my convulsive body, every shaking inch. I am sore crying when they charge up the stairs, hurling open the door, asking what the hell's the matter? Neither raised a fist, for I wept so much that it silenced them. Did you stuff yourself with a rubbish feed of sweets? Did you drink that milk? We think it's sour anyway. It must have turned your stomach. Don't fret about spilling it. We will have to dump it down the sink. Better change your pyjamas, we'll get the bed sorted. Did you eat something rotten? Or did something happen? Tell us. There was a noise before you came in. We heard it but couldn't place what it was or from where it came. Is that what ails you? But I say nothing. Not a single word. For they know I will tell what they want to hear. A lie. I say, no – I was just in a panic in case you noticed. Noticed what? My rifle, I lost it. It's gone, the gun, remember you gave me for Christmas.

PERJURERS

He took the ground from beneath my feet. That's as true as I'm standing here. That's how shocked and shaken a state he was leaving me in, roasting in the heat of the warmest June day man or beast could remember in the county of Donegal.

What did he imagine he was up to? Weren't himself and his family, from the oldest neglected in a garret to the youngest mewling in its pram, all and sundry belonging to him, weren't they up to their arses in this? And here's me, the foolish fucker to go aid and abet them. Why?

Aid and abet, that's how they describe it, the guards, were they to be let in on these shenanigans. Didn't I do well to bite my tongue before blurting this out just as it hit me? Wasn't I the smart fellow to hold it in reserve? Instead– wait till you hear this – I said, for my sins, I did as you asked me. No, you did more than ask, more like you begged me, I told him.

I have never begged from man, woman or child in my

life, never pleaded he lied, his shallow face narrowing with every word spoken through his red lips.

You pleaded in court, I got back at him, you pleaded not guilty.

That's another matter, he insisted, court is a different state of affairs entirely. I never mentioned anything about courts.

But I have done so, said I, I am bringing up this very subject, and all I warn you is that it might be wise if you find a better answer than what you're fishing with now, my boyo.

Do not call me boyo, he said, don't address me or mine in such an insulting fashion. Don't try that caper, letting on you look down – you dare to look down your nose at us. There's only one bad weed present and correct here and that's yourself. You and your breed worked for us for years, doffing your caps at my father and grandfather. Don't think I'm going to let you forget that fact. We allowed you licence for too long and look where it's got us. Me here, listening to you threatening us with guards and innuendoes we owe you anything. That court escapade happened years ago. Don't stir it into being once more. If you feel tempted, things could turn very bad for you. That's a warning, very bad indeed.

But I sensed a bit of panic on his part. His face reddened from more than the sun.

I did not kill a woman though, I said very calmly, and I

waited for him to explode.

No, he sat there, cool and collected again, suddenly the big man ready for all life's surprises, coming in all directions, ready to swat them from him. Getting away with murder, or next to it, had changed him, that was clear. He might have dodged the blows earlier, but now he could take them all on the chin. So, he sat there beside me in the vehicle, not a sound out of him for ages, not stirring, not a move, just looking at me, bolder than brass, waiting for me to continue my party piece while he pulled on a Sweet Afton, not having the manners to offer me a cigarette from his near-full packet of twenty.

Are you going to contradict me? I challenged him, are you going to claim it never happened? The road accident, you, drunk as a skunk behind that wheel – you, not fit to clean your arse, let alone be in charge of a car? Are you going to deny that?

Not a peep out of him. Not a murmur. So I figured out he was going to let me blab my way onward. I knew damned well I should have watched my mouth. It was and ever will be as open as a gateway. He was well advised silence was the best policy for loosening my tongue and giving him all the ammunition I could provide. I'm the kind who cannot endure saying nothing – just cannot endure it for whatever reason, don't question me why. So I burst out, what have you to say to defend yourself?

Only one here needs defending, he retaliated, and it's

you, you louse. Do you think threatening me will change my mind? No, not this time. No amount of squirming will let you off this hook. You will pay in some shape or form what you owe my family. We've been fools enough to let you away with bleeding this business dry. We can take no more. There's plenty others of your ilk, in debt to us, they see you run riot, mocking us, they are already trying the same. We have to crush this way of working. A terrible example we've let you set. No longer, no more. We've permitted this to happen for the sake of old times and long connections, and here is the thanks we receive. Old scars ripped open, old wounds back bleeding, you thinking you have me and mine over a barrel—

I told the court a lie, I informed him, you got away with what you did, got clean away, and like it or lump it, you owe me for that. I don't deny we're owing you a few bob—

Jesus, you should know that chapter and verse, he said, know it to the nearest pound, shilling and pence, we have sent you enough bills and reminders.

What does it tally? I asked him, a few skittery hundred—

Thousands, he corrected me, we dealt in hundreds just after the war, twenty years ago, but this is the 1960s and the country's changing, the days of writing off all debts are gone, you have to face the music, we're now talking thousands, thousands you don't have, monies we will likely never see, if we are depending on your like to put his hand in his trouser pocket and pull out nothing but the drawers he's wearing, if he's wearing any.

I saved you from jail, my voice was close to shouting, and the sweat of the summer's heart was nearly blinding me, sweltering behind the wheel of the locked vehicle where he'd insisted on meeting me. I saved you – how long would a fancy nancy like you survive—

You're out of line there, he warned me, I have bedded more women in this county than you could shake a stick at. Less of that talk, he barked, but I had started and was going to finish.

Weren't you the family's infant, the last and loveliest of the breed? Didn't they ruin you? Mammy's favourite, spoilt rotten, didn't every dog and devil know that? Such rearing left you less of a man than you should be, soft as butter, certainly between the sheets. That's what the whores you panted after in these parts said about you—

I won't warn you again to cut that line of chat, he threatened, I could take on and finish off any bastard who might choose to go a few rounds, I could knock the lining out of you, give you the hiding you've long looked for, you thieving—

Maybe so, I smiled, but as I maintained before and always will maintain, I never killed an innocent human being. When you close your eyes, I asked, tell me this and tell me no more, do you ever see her face looking back at you, gazing behind the windscreen, before she's hurled through it? Do you hear it shatter? Breaking in pieces everywhere. Glass scattered all over the road. You shed all that spilt blood even your mammy and her parlour maids can't wash away.

She could open the car, walk out of it – she was able to ask what happened—

That's the story your brother spun to the judge, I reminded him, he had that version of events off pat, and he was believed. With your connections how could he not be?

We know whose side we're on, he said quietly, and you were once on the party's side as well, you and yours. That's why, under Jesus, we trusted the lot of you, fools as we were. Her husband, the dead woman – well in with the lads—

You were lucky he was, I announced, he did as he was ordered by the powers that be. He got himself into such a state he would not even testify, just nodding his head to all that was put to him. Still, but there were folk heard him crying that his wife was dying, lying like a broken doll by the side of the road, inconsolable he was then. Do you not still hear him wailing that Sunday evening when it happened at—?

Christ, how many accidents were caused at that particular black spot? he asked. This was only one of many.

But this was yours, I pointed out, and I helped you get

away with it. I was your witness, I swore under oath, I committed perjury, and now in return the least you can do—

Write off what's owed? Is that what you want? Well, you'll want. Chance after chance we've given you shower to pay us back, instalment after instalment. Every time you plead another type of poverty. If we kept on listening to your litany of woes, we'd be as down on our uppers as you are. We're not running a charity. A man should pay what he owes.

And you owe me, Bates, you owe me for staining my soul, I accused him. Getting me to swear to a confounded lie. You were like a rat up a drain pipe, I was your witness that we had no more than two halves of whiskey through the whole day. I did not say you staggered to your car—

There's the confounded lie, he argued.

Staggered to your car, and drove like a lunatic, I let him know, you showing off, your big head twice its normal size that you could down so much booze and get behind the wheel.

Lies, he repeated, more dirty lies. Lies.

Do you admit it was me who did as you bid me? Tell the court the lie, state you were an honest man, a sober fellow— I questioned him.

Wasn't all this hammered out years ago? Why persevere on what's been long forgotten? Who remembers that day and what happened? I don't recall it, he declared, and neither should you.

He does, the dead woman's husband, I said, he lost a wife, his wains lost their mother—

Wains? They were more or less grown women and men at that time, in their teens and twenties, he jeered at her memory.

A mother's still your mother, I let him know, no matter what age you lose her. Jesus, have you no heart in you? Do you treat this world and any unfortunate enough to have contact with you and yours as dirt? Sweep it away, forget—

I won't forget you and what you owe, he retaliated, I want that cash, or whatever else you can use to cover it.

It was then he may as well have put a bullet through me. I now knew why I was sitting next to him in the van on this blistering day. Why he wanted to meet where we did meet, what precisely he was after. I played the innocent. Look, how can I pay you that entire sum? I wondered. You no longer want me on the books. Do I work—

You no longer can work, he snapped.

My nerves, I explained, it's my nerves stopping me, I'm bad with—

Bad with nothing, he nearly spat on me, you're a lazy bugger, you always have been. My family, sisters and brothers, they've been foolish enough to buy this and every other excuse for the delays getting your account in order. Now they agree with me, we want you out. Why in hell should we not? Why should we heed your nonsense, giving you eternal leeway because you claim you committed perjury for my benefit—

Perjury, I said, that's what it was, I repeated, nearly roaring now.

Your word against mine, he threatened. And you agreed I was sober as the day was long the evening of that crash. Who's going to credit you changed your side of the story? All to suit yourself. What would the court or the guards make of that fine kettle of fish? Do you think they'd heed any nonsense about nerves – a grown man whinging he's not right in the head? How under Christ and his blessed mother could you be relied on to tell the truth? How would such a specimen hold down a job and do a day's toil? How could you be safe driving a vehicle?

I could hear what he was threatening. At the worst of times it was always what I dreaded happening. Jesus, don't do that to me, I implored, don't drive off—

I have to, if you are to settle the bills outstanding, he calmly answered, just hand over the keys, get yourself out of here and let me take this crock off your hands. I'll do you that last favour and no more will be said about the remainder—

Don't do that to me, not on the town street, you may as well strip me bare, I confessed. We've always held our heads high in this town. Once upon a time, my family, we ran four businesses—

Then you should have known better than to ruin them. The keys, give! he snapped.

I handed my keys to him.

He lifted them into his hand. Count yourself lucky you live in a council house, he spat in my direction, or you would be on the streets.

I have a wife, you know, I reminded him, a wife and children. That's my son's name painted beside mine on the side of the van, three youngsters, the eldest son starting secondary school, my wee girl adores me and the smallest still an infant, would you evict them—

Don't try that caper, it's you who's evicted them, should that arise, he reminded me. Are you crying? Are you actually sitting beside me, crying like a cat? Is this now what I'm dealing with? What kind of funny boy are you? You are quick to christen me the nancy – what about yourself? A grown man, smelling of his own shame. Is that what's become of you? Whinging?

But I couldn't stop, I couldn't.

Pull yourself together, he advised, clean your face, dry your eyes and walk away. As I've said, no more will be asked for – what point looking? Blood from a stone anyway.

How will we manage? I heard myself asking him.

Borrow from the one of your brothers who's made a fair few bob, he told me. Get him to deliver the handouts we're sick pouring in your direction. And there's work on the boats in Killybegs. Aren't you always singing your own praises about your prowess in a fishing vessel? Isn't it, as you claim, in your blood?

When I was a young man, I explained myself, I then had age on my side—

Another excuse for doing nothing, one excuse after another, he said. You'd sicken a dog, skiving. Start looking for work today. If it has to come to it, head across the water. Birmingham. Haven't you brothers married in Birmingham?

They would be good to me, I said, frightened I was going to start bawling again, for going to Birmingham, to England at all, working on the roads, navvying, that scared the living daylights above all else out of me, for these lads that laboured with my brothers might well be the best in the world, but they're rough men.

Away you go then, best of luck, he wished me. And before you leave, you should know I reckon you did not commit perjury. You just did as you were told. For once in your life, you did as you should. Get out of the van. Go.

I went.

The town looking at me, I stood on my own, watching him drive off, my pride, my joy, taking my living with him. And I remembered, since he denied it, I had saved his bacon, because, once upon a time, for him I had committed perjury. I admit that charge, me standing there as the sun was splitting the stones of the street, wondering where in hell was I to turn now. Who would take me? Tell me where? Who?

RED

id you see our son?

This is his photograph. Him on a rooftop. He wears a blindfold. He is aged fourteen years. Do you notice his hands? His soft, unlined hands. They are tied, tied behind his back. I think he is pushing them, the three men, the killers, taking them on, those holding him by the arms, the cowards who gang up on a child, our son.

In this second picture, he is falling.

Falling to the ground, flying, like a bird – no, not like a bird, birds escape to the sky. The sky watches him falling, our boy, and it does not save him, the bird held in my arms, cradled in my hands, his beating heart, his wings, broken – that is him falling.

I close my eyes to watch him more clearly, as he was, alive, and so he appears as he was, as he always will be, before he died.

These photographs, do not ask how I came across them. Money was involved. Money is always involved. It must be. I needed to buy them. They show me what has happened. Without them, how could I know? How could I understand what they did to my son? My only son.

So, let me hang my head. Let me not hear. Let me not say what they want me to say. What they would say to me. This son, this precious son whom you lament sorely, what was he? He stained his soul, he soiled his body sleeping with his own kind. He took and he gave to others dangerous drugs, charms of the devil to lure our young men to his filthy ways. He fouled our streets, our city, our country, our faith. Is this the son you mourn? For him you want revenge – this lump of dung dirty dogs would not smell, let alone touch?

Yes, I want revenge. Revenge for my son being taken to a rooftop. Revenge for the curses heaped upon his head. Revenge for the child innocent of all their accusations. But what chance have I of getting that? What am I?

A man now grown old before his time.

A man whose heart will cease beating soon, eaten – raped by sorrow, devoured by anger, a man who wanders, weeping with his wife, his three daughters, banished from their home, in exile, hungry for the day I can lead our men to the demons, those who slaughtered my boy, my blameless child, neighbours they once were, now my sworn enemies, for I know who they are, where they lie hidden, those who did the deed.

Why did they do it? Why pick him for their attention?

Who was he?

He was fourteen years old. They led him to the rooftop. They threw him from it. Spare me seeing him fall from it. He is still falling – spare me seeing it.

I know who they are. I will lead my avengers to each and every house they hide in, but I know where they can be found, those who declare my boy did not deserve to live, and when I find them, marked by his guiltless blood, I will do unto them as they have done to mine. I will not sleep again until I see them falling, falling – do not let me see my child falling – that is what I live for, to witness how they'll suffer, to hear they died as my child died.

How did they do this?

They came to our door, the door of the house now abandoned. They knock, and we answer, my youngest girl clinging to my legs, her older sisters guarding their mother, fearless like herself.

They stand there, at one time our neighbours, we must now call them the police, they insist. The police of God, they are on patrol, they are searching for—

Who are they searching for? Heretics and infidels, homosexuals.

So they say, but they are lying. No, they are looking for children. They say, your son, we want him.

He is not here, his mother lies, and they strike her. Our daughters scream. I am not allowed hold them, nor can I comfort my wife.

Why do you want him? I ask.

We need him, they reply.

Why?

To answer our questions.

He is our only son.

All the more reason for him to die of shame, shame brought on himself and on all in this house. We know about him.

Know what?

He is steeped in such evil we cannot tell you before his mother and his sisters – before his father, if that same father fears God.

And you, you fear God? My wife points at them, what do you know about my son? How do you know it?

They do not answer her, but turn instead to me.

What do you truly know about your son? they ask.

He stays at home, I tell them. He avoids rough company. He reads. He goes to school.

Does he play games? Does he watch sport? Does he offend God looking at men and women nearly naked insulting our Maker—

He is kind to his mother and sisters, he respects me, his father, I insisted to them, why do you want to take him?

Does he help his mother with her work in the house? They want to know.

He has washed dishes, when she asked, I inform them.

Does he spend much time with his sisters?

He is their only brother, they love him, they sing with him—

Sing what?

Our songs, our tribal songs, why should they not? I demand to know.

He is then, in your opinion, a gentle fellow? Would you yourself describe him so?

And I recognise the threat. I know what they imply. What they will kill him for. No matter what I say, it will convince them more to take him from us, to lead him to jail, to carry him to the rooftop, to maim his lovely limbs, to watch him, falling, falling, falling …

We need him for a few hours, they explain.

He's done nothing wrong.

Then you've nothing to fear.

Why are you taking him? His eldest sister dares to inquire.

Ask your brother, they reply, your quiet, helpful, gentle, singing brother, but do not expect him to tell you—

Are you telling us he has sinned? His mother wants to know. We have all sinned, she asserts.

But not as he has, they shout in her face, we are wasting time. Give him to us now.

They took my boy then. My quiet boy. Who never sinned. Unless they made him.

We waited to see him – each morning from then on, myself, my wife, his mother and father, we went, we asked to see him. We wanted to gather him, our frightened boy, in our arms, bathe him clean of dust and dirt, bring him home to us and to his sisters who were weeping day and night for their lost only brother.

Each morning we were told the same, unchanging story. Tomorrow, come for him tomorrow.

Tomorrow came, another tomorrow – come the next day, they kept ordering us to do. Are they laughing at us? my wife whispered. Are they mocking? These men, perhaps they mock, I told her, but they do not laugh. Is our boy even with them? She wondered. Ask them – ask – ask.

I feared doing so, I feared knowing what they might tell me. And so they told me, he is not here. Not any longer. He has been sent away.

To where? Where have you sent my child?

My wife's voice shocked me. She so quiet, so respectful, so obedient, now spoke like thunder. And they answered to her face, Tabqa, he has been sent to Tabqa.

This news silenced us. It silenced them. There had been word of what happened in Tabqa. We all knew what that word was. They could not look at us. The warriors of God made that decision, they lied. We must make preparations to go to Tabqa, I told them, but my wife, she said, where – where in Tabqa?

Natka 11, one replied.

The death cell, my wife accused him.

The security unit, where justice is dispensed—

Without a judge, without any judge, my wife said in her lowest voice.

It was as if this woman I no longer knew, as if she, my wife, had struck those men. They had expected her to scream, to weep, me to control her, but she had no need for restraint. She told them calmly, I know where he is. She told them carefully, I know who you are, I know what you will do to my child, and I know that God knows what you are doing.

Then you had better see him soon, they advised us, see your sinner of a son.

We are all sinners, I said, and someday—

We will all pay for what we do, my wife said.

See him soon, I'll say no more, our tormentors advised us.

There is a river in this city. The sacred river of the Euphrates. There is a jail beside that river, and in that jail there is a cellar, a basement. From her eyes my wife shed the waters of the Euphrates when she saw our boy, our son, our good child seated in a chair, tied to it, wearing white shorts that blood had stained, a red football jersey torn about his body, his thin back and belly, men with guns at either side, men with masks, where he sat, shaking.

He is the baby in my arms, who cannot sleep, crying. I cannot take him to me, cannot stop him crying, cannot comfort my weeping son, his mother on her knees, her hands out to the men, begging – begging for what?

The sounds she speaks make no sense.

Perhaps they are not words – she the most strong, who barely sighed giving him birth, she most sure in the service of God, sure he will save our child, she cannot speak, she howls instead.

I hold her as she holds me, for we are not allowed to touch our son who is now calling, Daddy.

Daddy, daddy.

Daddy, daddy, daddy.

I take my wife's hand, I raise her from her knees, I lead her to my son. She will defy their masks and guns. She does, holding our son, we place our arms about him, let them fire their weapons, let them kill us all. We will die together.

They want money, my boy says, all they want is money. Find them money, pay them money, I will get out of here then. Money, pay them.

I touch his wet face, I kiss his drenched cheek. Let them kill me for doing so. Why do they not shoot me? But of course, they would not do that. They wait for my answer. Will I pay them money?

I say, do not worry, it will be all right. But I have no money.

My son does not know that. His guards do not either. One says, smiling, a day or two, you can have him back, your son. But I know we will not. I, my wife, we now must wait for word. It comes days later.

He arrives to our family, to our home in Raqqa. The official tells us our son is dead. Killed, according to the law that all his like must perish. He has been taken to a building with three storeys. He has been hurled from the rooftop. An addict, they accuse him, my child who did not even smoke a cigarette in this life. A boy who looked at men to lead them astray, they further accuse him, in his red jersey and shorts, he is an offence to God.

So they condemned him to die, the crowd watching. Did they say anything to save him? My wife wants to know.

The official does not answer.

Did they say anything? Did anyone—

There is no record, if they did, he tells her.

So they were all like you? Your kind? Your kind that murders children, innocent children, singing, playing football? Get out, she tells him, go murder more boys—

He fucked his own kind, the official roars at her.

And for that, she roars back, he deserved—

What was done to him and to his like, cocksucker. The man's voice grows silent. As he stands before my son's mother, she punches him between his legs. He shrieks. No man nor woman has ever dared do that. In his shock, he even cries out – is it to his own mother?

She can no longer hear you, my wife spits at him, no mother now will hear you, you will die crying for her but all you will hear back is my curse on your cruel head.

With my dying breath, I will look and see you with my son's eyes, what demons you serve, he knows whose cock you suck.

He moves to the door, he hisses at me, control your womenfolk, all you have to do now is collect his corpse, your own cocksucker.

My three daughters see him to the door. They open it, lest his hand touches it. They watch him leave. He turns to the eldest. He asks, pray for me. No, she says. No. She closes our door. We will walk together, the three of us, she says, we will see our brother's body.

And so we go to find where they have left our son lying. It is in the morgue here in Raqqa. Wounds all around his lovely face and head. Bones broken to marrow, every part of him. I can hear them breaking, I can see him falling, I do not want to look, but I hear my daughter asking, why is his throat cut? Why has a knife pierced his back?

The doctor in charge backs away from the girl. My wife then asks, what happened? What did the crowd see? Who was there watching? Her voice demands that the doctor answer her. She terrifies him into telling what the ambulance driver that brought our son to hospital reported.

Three of the guards hauled him to the highest storey. Your boy fought them for his life, brave as a lion. They could not pin him down. He might get away, so one of the warriors stabbed him in the back. Even after they threw him to the earth, he still would not die, your son.

What was to be done? The soldiers of God discussed their dilemma. They pushed him into an ambulance. Then one stepped in – he was a foreigner – he cut the boy's throat.

The ambulance, red with his blood.

The rooftop, red with his jersey.

The city, red with children.

The country, red with my revenge.

This is his photograph. That is him on the rooftop. He wears a blindfold. He is fourteen years old.

His hands tied – tied behind his back.

He is not flying.

He is falling.

Falling.